Trigger Warning

— A Novel —

Robert Klose

Published by Open Books

Praise for
***Trigger Warning* by Robert Klose**

"This book has it all: hair-raising suspense, love after loss, hot-button issues of the day and, my favorite, legal thrills! Having been an adjunct professor, I can say this is must reading for everyone in academia including students and parents. Put it on Joe College's Summer Reading List!"

— James H.K. Bruner, Esq., author of *The Bike Cop* Series

"Not since Jane Smiley's *Moo* have we had such an entertaining and charged investigation of the strange ways of academia. While Robert Klose's *Trigger Warning* begins as a riff on academic politics, it quickly turns darker and more frightening. A grieving beloved teacher and a difficult student clash in a taut story that explores the complexity of human relationships, as well as the pressures and perils of surviving in a modern academic institution. Come for the story, stay for the compassion and the characters."

— Richard Cass, author of the prizewinning Elder Darrow jazz mysteries and *The Last Altruist*

"A cautionary tale about the hyper-politicization of modern academia and trigger warnings imposed on seemingly inoffensive curricula—subjects on which the author is well-informed. An intriguing and suspenseful story where the real antagonist isn't immediately apparent."

— John R. Cobb, author of *Tales of The Cemetery Trees*

"Robert Klose's *Trigger Warning* leads us unwittingly into the disturbing world of academia, then makes us experience the insidious tactics of the administrative 'powers that be,' that tighten around us until we can barely stand it."

— Cynthia Thayer, author of
We're Going Home: A True Story of Life and Death

"*Trigger Warning* by Robert Klose is an imaginative and engaging literary page-turner that takes a deep dive into the current state of academic politics and how higher education, and academic and intellectual freedom, have all become threatened by college and university administrators far more concerned with fiscal growth and student retention than dedicated to guiding students to develop critical thinking skills that prepare them to be citizens of a democracy. This story is told by an author who knows first-hand how corrosive this trend has become. *Trigger Warning* is as relevant as it is a pleasure to read."

— Bruce Pratt, author of *The Serpents of Blissfull*

"*Trigger Warning* gives us a fascinating view into the changing world of the university and touches on key issues of our times, but most of all is an engrossing tale filled with vivid characters that I came to care deeply about."

— John Bragg, award winning author of *Exit 8*

Published by Open Books

Interior design by Siva Ram Maganti

Cover image © Spiroview Inc shutterstock.com/g/peterspiro

For Mikal
who made me laugh

"University politics are vicious precisely because the stakes are so small"

—Henry Kissinger

ONE

While his wife was alive T was never lonely. Olivia was the only woman he had ever loved. She had kindled in him a belief that there was only one other person on God's earth who was meant to be his life's companion. He couldn't imagine being with anyone else.

T shuddered when he considered that meeting Olivia had been purely circumstantial, that their paths might never have crossed, or that somebody else might have "claimed" her had he not attended that faculty meeting with its uninteresting agenda. She had been a new hire and had noticed him rolling his eyes when the dean uttered one of his inanities. Then she smiled at him, which T found to be a courageous gesture for a rookie teacher—commiseration at first sight! T had blushed, not knowing what to make of the attention from this beautiful woman. He was not known as a wit, but he was astute: he recognized that Assistant Professor Olivia Killibrew saw something in him, and he certainly saw something in her. In short, they met, they dined, they spent long evening hours talking, just talking. Three months later they were married. Her first words after the small, quiet ceremony were, "I really do love you." His were, "Wonders never cease."

All of that was thirty years ago. Now she was dead and he was sixty-five. Did that mean he was old? He moved restlessly about the house with tremendous deliberation, conscious of every footfall. After her passing, he developed the habit of talking to the cat as he puttered. Tootsie (the name was Olivia's idea), for her part, spent a good deal of time staring at T, as if recognizing that something had changed but not, of course, knowing what that something could be.

Tymoteusz Tarnaszewski. Second-generation American. His parents had somehow managed to emigrate from communist Poland, jettisoning their Old World allegiances along with most of their belongings when they washed ashore in Boston like flotsam, holding toddler Tymoteusz by the hand. Early on, when he was learning English in the lower grades and frustrating his American classmates with his consonant-laden name—his father had forbidden that he introduce himself as "Tim"—he had acquired the nickname "T." It might as well have been tattooed onto him because it accompanied him through his personal and professional life. And now, in the wake of Olivia's passing, he felt as if he were shrinking, becoming an abbreviated version of the man he once was. "T" was little more than a breath sound.

After Olivia's death, he felt increasingly grateful for his teaching position at Skowhegan College in the heart of the North Maine woods. If nothing else, it was a distraction. If not for the demands of the teaching life, he couldn't see himself doing anything other than secluding himself at home and thinking of Olivia, as if thinking about her hard enough could somehow bring her back. He feared that, no matter how hard he thought about her, or how often he reminded himself that he had loved her, she would, eventually, adjourn from heart and mind and become an abstraction, like his parents' tales of relatives in the old country. Then he would truly be alone.

His parents were long gone, and he had no siblings. However, both of them had lived long enough to witness the ascent of their son, their boy from the communist Polish sticks, to the hallowed ranks of the American professoriate. The day Skowhegan hired him was one of the very few times he had seen his father cry. He also recognized that the old man wasn't crying for his son's success, but rather for the vindication of his own belief that one could triumph over the disability of communism by demonstrating, vicariously, that individual initiative—and tireless prodding by a dedicated mother and father—mattered in a place like America.

If there was any grace associated with Olivia's death it was that it happened early in the summer. This relieved T of the burden of coping with, and displaying, that first, fresh bout of acute grief during the teaching year. It also relieved him of the bitter duty of acknowledging false gestures and statements of sympathy from colleagues who otherwise paid him little mind. By the time school rolled around, Olivia's death was old news and few condolences were expressed. Life went on.

Yes, he was grateful for his teaching position, but he had no illusions about ever really fitting in due to his solitary and independent ways. Oddly, he still had an accent because his father had rigidly enforced the speaking of Polish at home. This made one or two of his colleagues suspicious of him. Clive Gridley over in Political Science called him "Russki," even addressing him as such at faculty meetings, always followed by a self-indulgent chuckle. T had quietly informed Clive that he didn't appreciate the attempt at humor and that he was Polish by birth, not Russian. But Clive, an arch Republican, only waved the comment away with the riposte, "Polack, Russki, what's the difference?"

T's father would have explained the difference in no uncertain terms. The man had a ferocious temper which he kept on a short leash. T knew that he could report Clive's jabs as harassment, but he chose not to. Knowing that other faculty members recognized the childishness of Clive's behavior seemed sufficient, although T sometimes wished they would say something in his defense. Maybe they weren't willing to defend a man who wasn't willing to defend himself.

Standing in stark contrast to this reticence was T as teacher. He was, in a word, superb at the task. His was the only class at Skowhegan where the students applauded the lectures. They applauded not only his style, his passion, and his uncanny narrative gifts—he spoke with a warmth and familiarity suggesting that he had actually known Charles Darwin—but the sense he generated that he cherished them. T had long ago learned that if the students knew that you cared about them, they would go to the ends of the earth for you.

The anecdotes were plentiful. There was the young man who

repeatedly came late to class because he could afford either food or gas—but not both—and kept running out of the latter en route to school. T bought his food for the remaining eight weeks of the semester. There was the young woman struggling to change a flat tire in the rain. T led her back to the driver's seat, gave her a handkerchief so she could dry her tears, and tended to the task himself, laboring away in the downpour until, at the end of his exertions, he looked like a drowned rat. And then there was the single mother who had brought her crying infant to class. Without breaking his stride, T had taken the child—who immediately quieted—and held him while continuing to discuss the transportation of molecules across the cell membrane. There were numerous other cases, but they all had one element in common: once T had extended his helping hand, he admonished the students, "Please keep this quiet." He just didn't want to draw attention to himself, and he had always had a problem with accepting gratitude.

And so the days peeled away. Earlier in his career, he'd had a productive research program, examining the embryological development of marine invertebrates. Once he received tenure, however, he felt free to acknowledge that he was, at best, a middling investigator and would never "discover" anything that would advance the general state of learning or be of value to anyone. And so he decided to circle the wagons around the thing he did best, the thing he loved: teaching. His lectures had always been worth attending, but once relieved of the persistent headaches associated with dividing his time between research and pedagogy, he caught fire, and, as the saying goes, people—his students—came from miles around to watch him burn.

TWO

September 1. The first day of classes. T loved the beginning of a new teaching year, not least because he didn't yet have any papers to correct or issues to deal with, so he could enjoy, simply enjoy, getting to know his students. Earlier in his career, Skowhegan had been a moderately selective school—the students who won admission had done generally well in high school and brought considerable tools and talent with them to college. But about fifteen years back there was a sea change and, seemingly overnight, T found himself teaching at an open admissions institution. The higher-ups attributed the altered policy to an altruistic desire to be more "accessible," but T had his own idea: there were fewer college-age students around and just too many damned colleges struggling to survive. The result was that the talk in recruitment circles turned from "young scholars" to "warm bodies." But when this was deemed unkind and politically delicate, the administration circled back, with a gloss, and decided to refer to Skowhegan students as "rising scholars." T, for his part, knew better.

The upshot was that, with open admissions, the student body had become uncommonly heterogeneous. Some of them were quite bright and talented and T had no problem thinking of them as scholars. But there were also those with poor skills: they could neither write nor cipher nor process scientific terminology and concepts in anything but the most rudimentary manner. Some, in their frustration at their lack of comprehension and progress, became hostile. T found himself, the holder of a Ph.D. from Boston University, teaching many of his students in a remedial fashion, which absorbed a tremendous amount of time and yielded little in the way of results. He recalled once giving a quiz on which a student received a grade of minus-one out of ten. When she protested that such a grade was impossible, T quietly drew her attention to the fact that she had misspelled her own name. "If you correct it, I'll give you the point back," he told her. She immediately did so, which elevated her grade to a zero.

But there was an even more challenging subset of students that stupefied T: those who rejected empirical learning outright and chose instead to argue from the standpoint of emotion and hearsay. Such as the young woman who had risen in magnificent ire, right there in the classroom, when T had broached the topic of evolution. T recalled her words precisely: "For what you have taught today you shall be damned to the everlasting fires of hell."

So.

But what could he do? This is what higher education had become, and T wasn't sure the situation was different anywhere else, except perhaps at the Ivies. But even the Ivies had their issues to deal with. The venerable Harvard itself, for example, didn't know how to handle a faculty member whose research area was alien abductions.

Even when the teaching got frustrating, there was always the periodic boon of a sabbatical year to lean into. But even here T had run into a sticky wicket. Sabbaticals—available every five years to someone of T's rank—were originally intended for personal renewal: a year away from teaching and research to change one's direction, plumb a different set of interests, and return to the job much improved, raring to go and full of new ideas and insights. No longer. Now the colleges and universities wanted a concrete product related to one's field that would enhance the resources of the school in some material way. But T, on his last sabbatical, had spent the year at home, reading all the books he felt he should have read a long time ago. He returned to Skowhegan reenergized in body and spirit; but this wasn't enough for the dean, who fumed at the lack of material results. "Product!" he had barked, his hands outstretched, palms up, fingers flexing. "I must have *product!*"

That's when T, surprising even himself, laid a black-and-white speckled composition book on the dean's desk. "What's this?" the man had demanded, perplexed.

T answered quietly and clearly, "My reading journal. I read two books a week during my sabbatical year and took careful notes. There are some lovely titles here, with my reflections and insights. Perhaps some will be of interest to you."

Dean Roger Olib grew red and began to jibber. He knew that T knew that he wasn't a reader. He was a doer. A maker. He got things done. He had told the faculty as much at their first meeting when he had been appointed to his office three long years ago. T had gotten a quick read on the man and how poorly read he was. Which is why he was surprised when the dean quoted, of all people, the uber-literate Teddy Roosevelt. Slamming his hand down on the conference table, he had declaimed, "I do not have a first-rate mind, but I do have a capacity for action."

Oh, how T wished, how he wished, that the dean had stopped at that comma. But in the ensuing weeks, months, and years, Roger Olib had confirmed that first clause, demonstrating again and again that he did not have a first-rate or, for that matter, even a second-rate mind. Whether it was the idea of name tags for faculty and staff on the tiny campus, or the attempt to secure funding for a personal Segway so he could, as he put it, "be out among the people," or the policy to allow students with math anxiety to substitute swimming for algebra, the dean had become something of the village idiot, pursuing his inane initiatives and raging when he was unable to attract allies. As Clive Gridley—someone with whom T rarely sympathized—so cogently phrased it, "The man is a goddamn shame." Then he snorted.

T knew that the dean didn't like him, but, to paraphrase Clive, it was a goddamn shame the man couldn't do anything about it. T was senior faculty, a full, tenured professor. His position was cast in iron and he was, for all intents and purposes, an immovable object, a chronic source of pique for the dean. But the upside of the arcana of the academy was that there were so many protections in place—for everybody—that dropping a student from a class, reducing the hours of a janitor, or, above all else, getting rid of a tenured professor, was a labor of Sisyphus. A college campus was a warm wallow in which some performed their duties conscientiously, while others luxuriated in their sense of invulnerability. T thought about the French instructor, Ted Toth, also sixty-five years old, but long burned out. He routinely canceled his classes, citing professional conflicts, when it was common knowledge that he was fiddling around on his boat in Birch Harbor. Oddly, he had never discerned this as the reason his colleagues had nicknamed him "Boats." The conventional wisdom was that it was easier for the university to allow him to live out his days than to try to dislodge him for malingering, which would be a long, hard, expensive slog, bringing the union out in full force. It was, simply put, cheaper to keep paying the man and acknowledge that students just didn't care when a faculty member didn't show up for class. In fact, they were generally delighted.

At the other end of the spectrum were those for whom the college was their life's breath. They gave all they had as if the fate of humankind depended upon their exertions. This was personified in Praveen Khatri over in math. Eighty-five years old—eighty-five!—and still at it, and with all the dedication of the new hire fresh off his dissertation. He had come to Skowhegan fifty years ago when T was a sophomore in high school fretting over his frog dissection.

T knew he was somewhere north of the middle of this continuum. In his almost forty years of teaching, he had canceled only one class, but only because he had spun off an icy Maine road into a snowdrift. Truth to tell, that incident had left him with a subtle sense of loss. This reflected his compulsive nature: his attendance in the classroom had been perfect, and suddenly, it wasn't. T brooded for weeks over what he considered his failing. There were moments when he still did.

T was not as dedicated as Praveen Khatri, but he was dedicated. He took his teaching seriously, and although the students, in their deficiencies and lack of preparedness, were becoming more challenging to teach as the semesters and years wore on, T had learned to nurture those few clever ones who were quick studies, and for whom bright futures waited. These were the students who lingered after class to talk, just talk to him about not only the course material but their hopes and dreams. It was sweet, and T knew that, at root, he loved them. And since Olivia's death, he knew that he needed someone to love.

THREE

T WAS UNPREPARED FOR the drama that would ensue as September turned to October. It all developed rather slowly, like the opening of a flower. In retrospect, he should have anticipated it. The theme had been in the news for years. It was naive of him to think that Skowhegan College was somehow immune.

The announcement came at a meeting of the Faculty Assembly. The president of the college, Ned Trumbull, would be in attendance in the small lecture hall. Grave and measured in his speech, he had been at Skowhegan for five years—an eternity in the peripatetic life of professional college presidents—and was still, in T's mind, inscrutable. T tried hard to think of a single initiative that the man had proposed or a single utterance of substance. The two of them had never had a one-on-one conversation. He was convinced that the president didn't even know his name. So his presence at the assembly was something of a curiosity, like the Wizard of Oz stepping out from behind his curtain. A pot was clearly on the boil.

When T entered the room everyone was chattering. A few paused to acknowledge him and exchange pleasantries. "How's your semester going, T?" "Hey, do you have this Jiffer kid in class? He's already got a degree. What the hell is he doing here?" "I heard something nice about you today." But when T inquired as to what that might be, the colleague wrinkled her nose and turned away.

Instruction at Skowhegan was provided by a nice round figure of fifty faculty. For nine hundred students. Not a bad ratio. T took a seat next to Magda Zweck, one of the clinicians from the Counseling Center, who displayed her affection for him by hooking his arm and squeezing. "Are you excited?" she inquired.

T looked at her with something resembling subdued amusement, examining her face, as if he could discern some meaning there. He couldn't. Excited? Was Magda privy to something? Only one way to find out. "Magda, do you know what this is all about?"

The attractive, fiftyish woman with cowlicked, salt-and-pepper hair shrugged and then shook her head. "No, but it must be something."

T should have realized there was no nuance there, no deeper meaning to excavate. Magda—whom he genuinely liked—was simply perpetually sunny. He supposed she had to be to handle everything she dealt with. Appropriately, she was rigidly tight-lipped about her corner of campus, due to the level of confidentiality her job required. T sometimes mused at the result if she could somehow be pried open. Oh, what stories she could tell.

President Trumbull walked in, bright red bowtie blazing beneath his ashen countenance, wire-rim bifocals perched on the tip of his nose. Dean Roger Olib followed in his wake, slightly bent, as if in obeisance to a higher power. The chattering died down and all heads turned forward. Trumbull was wearing his trademark expression of perpetual disappointment, pursed lips and all. Magda leaned over to T and whispered, "Here we go!" T stared at her again.

T found himself wondering what Trumbull would look like if he smiled. There was a pronounced sadness about the man as if he were constantly on the brink of announcing that someone had died. The drawn face, long wisps of gray hair, and reluctance to look you in the eye when he spoke, all portrayed someone who always seemed to be somewhere else. Which led T to ponder how much the president's heart was in his job at Skowhegan. Well, it must have been to some extent, given his five-years-and-counting tenure. But then again, maybe, as Clive Gridley had once chided, he was in the witness protection program. "What better place to be anonymous?" he had added with a self-indulgent snort.

Trumbull stood at the lectern, arranging his papers and then adjusting his bowtie before saying "Good morning" without looking up as if he were pronouncing a death sentence. In unison, the faculty chanted, "Good morning!"

Without preamble, the president began with, "We have had an incident."

Magda leaned against T, who returned the gesture by exerting some counterpressure. They glanced at each other, and T noted for the first time that her eyes were blue.

"A student," continued the president, "who shall of course be nameless for considerations of confidentiality, has filed a complaint. My impression, after careful investigation, is that the complaint is valid."

Trumbull's delivery was ponderous, the work of a man in cement shoes trudging through a field of mud. This was all so peculiar. Wasn't a student complaint a matter to be handled administratively between the student and other interested parties? Why this convocation?

The president continued. "From this point on, all faculty are directed to continuously review the content of their courses and, as necessary, either excise material that could legitimately be deemed threatening to a student's sensibilities, or include appropriate trigger warnings."

A hum ran through those gathered. Trumbull raised his eyes and peered over his bifocals. This was gesture enough from the sphynx to bring silence to bear. "I don't know why this would alarm anyone. Quality control is in everyone's interest."

T glanced around at his colleagues, searching for some sign that somebody knew what was going on. What was the backstory? There must be some backstory. Seeing no sign that anyone was about to speak up, T—who rarely raised his voice at meetings—got to his feet and waved a hand for attention. "President Trumbull…"

Roger Olib, who was seated behind the president, got up as well. "No one is asking for questions at this point," he said. "Sit down, T."

"Sit down, T? Is that an order, Roger?" T couldn't believe it. It was as if he were observing an alternative version of himself, an assertive, self-assured, alternate version capable of pique. He wondered what Magda Zweck was thinking of him at that moment.

The dean seemed to relish the confrontation. The corner of his mouth turned up as if he were trying to suppress a smile. "Yes," he said, staccato. "Sit. Down. The president hasn't finished speaking. There will be time for questions later."

T settled back into his seat. He felt mortified. But why? He was more than an intellectual match for Roger. But there was further reason for his mortification: not one of his colleagues had cheered him on. There was no groundswell of support. He suspected that, true to form, they would approach him in private and tell him how right he was. How very right.

T stole a glance at Magda Zweck, who was regarding him with those blue eyes. T knew the look; it was the same one she employed when listening to a student lament. It was the look that said, "It's not you, it's them. You are blameless; it's the world that's at fault."

T bristled at that look and the pity it communicated, but his attention was captured once again by the drone of the president's voice. "To ensure this quality control," he continued, "all syllabi will, from this point on, be carefully reviewed by the provost, who will make suggestions for abridgment or the incorporation of trigger warnings."

It suddenly became crystal clear to T. Some student had objected to something some professor had said in class or to some item of course material. The question now was, who could it be? T scanned the faces in the room, but he could discern no evidence of guilt. No matter, it would come out. Having a Ph.D. was no bulwark against the timeless practice of gossip.

Contrary to the dean's statement, no time was set aside for questions. T looked on, dumbfounded, as the president picked up his papers, turned, and left the room, with Roger Olib scurrying in his wake like a border collie.

The faculty began to chatter again. Ted Toth came up behind T and patted him on the back. "Nice try, T," he said, nodding. "I'm sorry they shut you down."

T managed a cursory, "Yes, thanks, Boats." And then, after a pause, "I'd be interested in your take on this new policy."

The French professor began to fumble in the pockets of his sports coat, as if the answer might be there, on a slip of paper perhaps. And then he stammered, "Well, er, the key is not to rush to judgment. My experience is that when one thinks about these things they invariably turn out to be benign."

"And we roll merrily along," said T, putting a coda on his colleague's prevarication.

Ted's eyes brightened. "Yes," he said, raising a finger. "Yes, that's it exactly." As he said this he made two fists, as if to demonstrate what he thought strength to be. "All of us have to put our shoulders to the wheel." Then he turned and left the room. T sensed which wheel Boats would be shouldering, given the predictable rhythms of Maine tides.

Magda Zweck, standing by T's side and smiling in an affirming manner, told him, "I do wish people would support you in public. Why are they so reluctant?"

T regarded his colleague. "Magda, I'd think that with all your skills you'd know the answer. Fear. The fear of confronting power, and of not being well thought of. The fear of associating with a loose cannon."

Magda was laser-focused on T. "Where do you think I fit in?" she asked, her smile gone now, her eyes boring through his gaze.

T smiled for both of them. "Let's have coffee soon. I don't think free association requires a trigger warning."

FOUR

It's peculiar, thought T as he made his way across campus to his office. But Boats was probably right. T had seen it time and again in his career—the college higher-ups proposing some initiative or other, which almost invariably bore no fruit and was soon forgotten. That's the way it had been with the "Healthy Treats" campaign when, overnight, all the soda disappeared from the vending machines, to be replaced with juices and high-density protein drinks. That lasted about a week before some observant student studying food science noted that the juices contained more sugar than the soda had, and so, in a wink, the much cheaper soda was back and the concept of healthy treats became a footnote.

As T came around the library, the campus green opened up before him. It was still warm enough for students to be lounging in shorts and sandals, throwing Frisbees and doing their exercises. The green was lined with red maples, the leaves slowly turning flame orange, as if someone had touched a match to them. T decided to cut across the green, if only to feel soft earth under his feet.

"Heads up!"

T turned and ducked as a Frisbee spun by. A male student, barefoot, came running up to him. "Sorry, Professor T," he apologized. T regarded him and smiled. The boy couldn't have been more than nineteen, with curly red hair and a mask of broad freckles. Even his skin seemed to exude red, which was only exaggerated by his deep blush. "It's okay," he said. "It's a sin not to be outside in this beautiful weather. Enjoy it."

"Will do!" said the student as he turned and ran off. T looked after him and noticed that even the soles of his feet glowed red.

T resumed his trajectory, smiling into his shirt collar. When did these students get so young? That's the problem with the teaching life, if you could call it a problem. Starting out, one is twenty-six or so, basically the same generation as the students. A few years later, though, one is thirty, but the students are still in their teens and early twenties. Then forty dawns, but they're still in their teens and twenties. Then comes fifty and sixty and, if one is both lucky and dedicated, like Praveen Khatri, there's no reason why one cannot persist into one's seventies and eighties. Except that, yes, the students are still in their teens and twenties. Is there a point when it all becomes too surreal? T thought that there must be. In his own case, he didn't understand much of what his students said when they spoke among themselves. He just didn't know the vocabulary. He often fantasized about what it would be like if someone, say Ben Franklin, were to materialize, and the first thing he heard was, "Shoot me an email or get me on Kik." What would he think?

It was serendipitous that, at this juncture in his thoughts, T would spot a slight, dark-skinned man sitting on a bench under one of the maples. T wasn't in a hurry, so he detoured. "Mind if I sit?"

Praveen Khatri looked up and smiled from under his gray tweed flat hat—the impossibly white, unblemished smile of an octogenarian who had apparently dedicated his life to the care of his teeth. He raised a small bunny paw of a hand and gestured. "Please. Yes, please."

T had always thought highly of Praveen. Like himself, the mathematician went about his business and made few waves. He also rarely spoke up at meetings and did just enough committee work to indicate that he was attempting to make contributions beyond the classroom. He was known as a kind, caring, and, above all—and this was important in math— patient teacher who spent hours of extra time outside the classroom, one-on-one, with students struggling with algebra or—God help us—calculus. And like T, he was a full tenured professor and so had a great deal of latitude to do things his way. And his way entailed the almost total eschewing of technology. He used his computer only for email, but otherwise gave his assignments on paper and expected the students to return their completed work in hard copy as well, which he corrected by hand. He had no cell phone and didn't seem worse for this deficiency. In fact, there was an oasis-like calm about the man, who had largely succeeded in constructing a life free of distractions.

T also knew there was a great sadness associated with Praveen. He was married, but his wife had remained in India all these years. The self-effacing Praveen never talked about such things, but in a small community it has a way of leaking out. The great mystery was why he had never brought her over. Or maybe he had tried but failed. In any case, it was known that he steadily sent the lion's share of his paycheck to her, and that he mounted an annual visit.

"I find it hard to be inside on a day like this. Do you agree?"

T smiled. "I don't find it hard to be inside teaching, but that meeting was no fun."

Praveen nodded. "Yes, it was painful," he admitted.

Curious word choice. T didn't think of the meeting as particularly painful. He would have said "frustrating."

"But," said Praveen, retrieving the thread, "meetings are one of the few times when faculty members get to be together in one place. So they have their purpose."

"Even if nothing comes of them," T was quick to add.

After a pause, Praveen noised, "One would hope." There was an odd note in the old man's voice.

"Do you think it's only the beginning of something? I don't think mathematicians have anything to fear. I mean, your business is numbers, and who could numbers offend?"

"You might be surprised."

T sensed that he was onto something. Praveen had turned away from him and was now staring wistfully into the distance. "Praveen, the one thing that wasn't mentioned at the meeting was who the culprit was."

Still looking away. "Culprit?"

"Wrong word. I mean, something happened in one of the classrooms. That's clear. It's only a matter of time until it comes out."

Praveen turned toward T. "Are you ready to be surprised?"

T regarded his colleague for a long moment. "I'm happy to listen."

Praveen put an arm around the back of the bench and drew himself closer to T. "You were wrong about numbers not being offensive. We live in an age when people actively seek offense where none is intended."

"Go on."

"You're right that it will come out, and since I have always considered you one of the most dedicated faculty members on campus, and with so much integrity, not to mention being a friend, I will tell you something."

T leaned toward his colleague, his look expectant.

"In fact, it's important that someone else know this before... what is that order called when a judge says you can't talk?"

"A gag order."

Praveen frowned. "What a terrible expression," he said, shaking his head. "But in any case, I teach a statistics course. It's not the most difficult math course, for two reasons. One, it's mostly formulas that one can look up. And two, one can apply it to so many interesting things, like sports, for example. But at the heart of statistics is a very important idea, and here it is: statistics has nothing to do with individuals, only populations. Do you agree?"

"Speaking as someone who got a B+ in statistics, I feel qualified to agree."

Praveen nodded approvingly. "It's too bad you weren't one of my students. You might have gotten an A."

T realized that, agewise, he could have been one of Praveen's students. "Or a C," he was quick to rejoin. "I understand you're a demanding teacher."

"There's nothing wrong with demanding quality work. Do you agree?"

"How can I argue with that?"

"I do like my students," said the old man, "but even parents become frustrated with their children on occasion. Just last week a young man gave me handwritten work I couldn't decipher. When I returned it to him, ungraded, and asked that he do what I had asked and type it, he became indignant. He said he would go to the dean." Praveen sighed. "But what can one do?"

"Did he go to the dean?"

"Yes, and Roger, to his credit, told the student that it was a matter between him and me, so I prevailed."

T wasn't about to let the conversation drift from its trajectory. "But back to statistics."

Praveen removed his glasses, squinted, and pinched the bridge of his nose. "Yes. My mind wanders these days. Not because I'm old, but because I find it pleasant."

"Populations," prompted T good-naturedly.

"Ah, yes. I was using college students in general as a statistical example. I had seen an article in the newspaper that stated that sixty-three point five percent of first-generation college students don't make it to graduation, compared to sixty-eight percent of second-generation college students who do."

"That sounds about right."

Praveen wagged a finger. "Not to one of my students. A young man sitting in the back row. At first I didn't grasp what was happening. I thought that he was getting ready to sneeze, but I soon saw that he was enraged. In fact, his body was shaking."

"Was he sick?"

"That's what I thought. As you might imagine, I don't get many emotional reactions in my math courses."

"Yes, it's not like poor Nan Hays in psychology. She runs a regular tissue factory over there. I'm sorry, I'm hijacking your narrative."

"I found it necessary to ask the student if something was wrong. He gathered himself and exploded. 'Yes,' he said, pointing at me. 'I am a first-generation student and you're telling me I won't graduate. You're trying to steal my hope.'"

T immediately recognized the inanity of that response. "But you weren't talking about him in particular."

"Of course not," said Praveen. "And that's exactly what I said. I explained that a population study had nothing to do with an individual's experience. Consider: the average American family has two point three children. Now I ask you, find me a family with that three-tenths of a child. Do you agree?"

"What happened next?"

"Another trip to the dean. But this time Roger saw it the student's way. He called me to his office and explained that I should have given the students a warning that I was about to say something some of them might be sensitive about."

"Or misinterpret."

Praveen brought a hand to his chin and brooded for a moment. "No," he said. "Not misinterpret. I've come to believe that we're teaching the students to view quantitative, scientific data as personal opinions designed to make them feel bad about themselves."

T sat back and regarded his colleague. He didn't think the old man had it in him to draw such a stark conclusion, given his reputation for quietude, compassion, and forbearance. But he didn't disagree with Praveen's assessment. It wasn't long ago that so-called "trigger warnings" were unknown. Then colleges began to prescribe them. Now the students themselves were asking for them. Or demanding them.

"What was the upshot of the meeting with Roger?"

Praveen sighed. "Do you understand now that the president was talking about me at the meeting? What could I do? I gave in. I apologized to the student and immediately revised my syllabus with asterisks indicating areas where they might have certain fears."

"There be dragons there," mused T.

Praveen threw him a doubtful look.

"Old maps," said T. "They had fanciful margins with images of sea beasts and other dangers, lest the ships stray too far from home."

Praveen nodded. He was no longer smiling. "Now my syllabus is adorned with those margins. I had no choice." And then, after a pause, "Do you agree?"

T heaved his own sigh. "No, Praveen. I like you and respect you, but I don't agree. You had nothing to lose by standing your ground.

You're a full, tenured professor. They don't dare harass you, considering your teaching reputation and what you put up with for the sake of the college."

Praveen slowly shook his head. "With all respect, my friend, you are wrong. There is always something to lose. I couldn't imagine saying no, I won't place these warnings in my syllabus. Wasn't it easier to just do it? I haven't had a complaint since."

"Yes, it was easier. But my question is, what now? What happens if you're asked to go to the next level and remove this material from your course?"

Praveen shrugged. "That's a hypothetical situation."

"Yes, it is. We're academics and we deal with hypotheses all the time. How else can we prepare ourselves for the possible?"

Praveen smiled. "That's why I like you. You have ideals. And energy. But do you think the administration won't come for you at some point?"

"No, I don't think they won't come for me. Forgive me, Praveen, but your giving in has put blood in the water. You've communicated to the higher-ups that they can get away with this nonsense. That they can cow the faculty. I think..." No, he wouldn't go on. He didn't want to chastise his colleague. "Listen," he said, warmly, "I'm sorry. Maybe it's my frustration that's speaking here."

Praveen touched T's arm. "Maybe I don't have the energy to fight. I'm eighty-five. At this point in my life, I have more salient concerns. Things that a man needs to think about and do before..."

T rested a hand on Praveen's shoulder. "I understand," he said. "I'm sorry you had to go through this. You, of all people. The faculty is aware of all the good you've done for these students, all the compassion you've shown them over the years." And then, mischievously, "I'm surprised a young female student has never taken an interest in you."

Praveen broke into a bright smile. "I wouldn't have responded," he said. "Statistically, ninety-eight percent of such dalliances fail. Why engage in something that can only bring more heartache?"

FIVE

More heartache. That's what Praveen had said.

T knew it was a fool's errand to compare heartaches, and yet, since Olivia's death, he couldn't help but acknowledge the heaviness that accompanied him like an entity. It sapped his energy, preoccupied his thoughts, and made him feel as if he were plodding through life, just trying to put one foot in front of the other. The thing was, Olivia had placed great emphasis on joy, not only in word but in the way she lived and moved in her space. T couldn't help but be inspired by it. He noted the way she interacted with her students, the genial way she contributed—and sometimes disagreed—at faculty meetings, and her uncommon gift for making others feel that they were the only ones who mattered when she was engaging them. She had a Socratic magnetism that drew people to her. Again and again T found himself asking,˙ *Why me? Why did she choose me?*

Only in her absence did he realize how much he had come to rely upon her in ways beyond the affective. He did a significant amount of writing for various natural history periodicals, the type of writing, he felt, that really mattered, if only because it offered an opportunity to get a human response from a broader audience. Early on he had written a few scientific papers, but there was something austere and alienating about those efforts. Perhaps it was the knowledge that few would read a paper titled, "Retrograde locomotion in *Paramecium caudatum*," and almost no one would trouble themselves to comment on it. No matter. Once T had been granted tenure he quickly gave up on laboratory and field research to write more creatively. There was subtle, as well as overt, blowback from the college: non-research pursuits did not garner the school its cut from successful grants. But T assuaged administrative frustrations by producing some truly beautiful pieces of writing on natural history which heightened Skowhegan's profile. However, he knew he wouldn't have succeeded to the extent that he had if not for Olivia, who could read a twenty-page paper in ten minutes and then come up with trenchant observations and recommendations.

T recalled an essay he had written concerning the partitioning of the feeding niche among two species of bees that favored an autumn variety of sedum. He was particularly proud of that piece and ran to Olivia like a third grader showing his mom what he had drawn in class. But when Olivia looked at it she brooded. Then she sat T down and told him, "Here's what I'd like you to do with this essay. Put it in a drawer and never look at it again. Now listen: writing this essay has taught you everything you need to know about doing it the right way. I want you to take those lessons and apply them to a subject that really interests you." And then, to lessen the blow, she produced an apple cobbler and poured the shell-shocked T a steaming cup of coffee.

T smiled when he recalled that episode. Her assessment had driven him into the confines of his home office, where he engaged in a writing *fuga del diavolo* for five days before producing a fanciful meditation on the secret life of mushrooms, which he laid before Olivia like a dog retrieving the morning paper for its master. This time he didn't hover, but rather left the house to go for a walk in the garden while she read his work. In truth, he didn't know what to expect. Just because one has worked hard on a project was no guarantee of quality or success. No one, he had long ago learned, was entitled to be published. But he didn't get far in this thinking. Just as he was examining the delicate purple petals of a coneflower, Olivia burst out of the house, waving his essay and whooping. She threw her arms around him and sang, "Exquisite! Don't cross another t or dot another i. Send it out now, and start at the top."

T's faith in Olivia's judgment was abiding. Three weeks later came the call from *The New Yorker. The New Yorker!* A check for five thousand dollars soon followed. It wasn't in T to toot his own horn, but Olivia had no such reservation. She placed an announcement in the college newsletter, informed the *Bangor Daily News* that a local boy had made good and, when no one at the next college meeting uttered a word of congratulations, she insisted they take a moment to acknowledge T's accomplishment. For his part, the mortified T reddened and struggled to avoid eye contact with his peers.

If not for Olivia, T wondered how he would be able to persist in that rarefied environment, so lacking in warmth. He suspected that there was something about him that just didn't sit well with people, although he felt himself to be generally well thought of. Maybe he was reaching too high and should have confined himself to small, obscure, non-paying outlets for his writing. Maybe he should have told his students not to announce their enthusiasm for his courses too loudly. Maybe he should not have accepted that teaching award. What was that metaphor? Crabs in a bucket. When one crab tries to climb out, the others claw him back down into the creeping, clicking mire.

And yet T needed to be working. If it weren't for the lectures, laboratories, tests, papers, meetings, and myriad student concerns and the interactions with administrators, what on earth would he do? Without Olivia, he needed to fill the void and allay the terrible loneliness. The thing, then, was to keep moving, stay involved, keep thinking forward, always forward. Having reached the milestone age of sixty-five, he couldn't help but wonder who in the college community was wishing he would retire. Thanks to laws forbidding age discrimination, the administration couldn't raise the subject with him, but some of his colleagues didn't hesitate. Clive the backslapper inquired, "So, when you gonna call it quits and join Boats on his yacht?"

T had stared at Clive's bright smile, behind which, he knew, the man was dead serious. At forty-five, he was in mid-career and still harbored dreams—or were they illusions?—of ascending the administrative ladder to clutch at the dubious power it offered. As such,

Clive knew that T's salary line could support the efforts of three or four adjuncts who would carry monumental teaching loads for low pay without the benefits enjoyed by tenure-line faculty. "I don't see retirement on the horizon, Clive."

The man's smile slowly faded. "Oh?" he said. "Why not?"

T wanted to say, "Spite," but he hung fire. "I'm flattered that you're interested in my welfare and personal happiness."

The smile completely evaporated. "Well," said Clive with a 'Gee, man, lighten up' shrug. "Just trying to make conversation."

"I'd prefer we talk about something else. I think I'm going to be around for a while."

T was actually quite willing to talk about where he stood on the trajectory of his career, but only with Olivia. Five years ago, before there was any indication of her sickness, they had observed his sixtieth birthday by taking a Sunday stroll on campus, walking hand-in-hand along the tree-line of maples. Most of the students were still in bed, leaving the campus sedate, silent, and bereft of hurrying bodies. They sat down on a bench, where T grew wistful. "It's hard to believe that I taught almost ten years here, alone, before I met you. I don't know how I did it."

Olivia had looked at him in mild disbelief. "Then as now you're doing what you love. Could you have imagined a better job?"

"I've often thought that I could be happy driving a bus."

Olivia laughed. "Of all things!"

T warmed to the topic. "Yes. I mean, when you drive a bus the people have to get on because it's in their interest to get to their destinations. But teaching is different. If a teacher has to cancel a class, the students cheer. I mean, they pay thousands to be here and yet they're happy when the product is not delivered."

Olivia didn't hesitate. "They wouldn't cheer if you didn't show up. They'd be concerned. In any case, you've just announced, in so many words, that you will be here for the rest of your life."

T threw her a questioning look. Even as he was examining her face for hidden meaning, he realized that she was right. Complaining—if that was what he was doing, however benignly—was a way of showing that he could take it and would continue to take it. "I do love it here," he said.

"Yes, you meet such interesting people."

SIX

Skowhegan periodically held so-called "TAR"—Teaching and Research —sessions, where folks got to present their research or talk about innovative teaching approaches. It was only once a semester, but T groaned when the announcement came that one was in the offing. The thing was, he found them painful at worst and uninteresting at best. Clive, for example, had given a presentation misleadingly titled, "Alternative Means of Achieving Learning Goals." After ten minutes, however, his talk had morphed into an indictment of left-leaning tendencies in the teaching profession. For some reason, he kept glancing at T, who had always kept his political sensibilities under wraps. The most uncomfortable moment came when Clive, in a faux gesture of conciliation, conceded that evolution should of course be taught in the biology curriculum, but the alternative point of view, so-called "creation science," should also be presented. "Balance," he said, holding his palms out and examining them. "Balance." T, for his part, had crossed his arms and firmed his lips.

And now another TAR event was on the horizon. Nan Hays would talk about accessing underutilized portions of the brain to enhance teaching performance. T didn't want to go, but it was a low-stress way of participating in campus life by simply showing the flag.

When he entered the small lecture hall, he was cheered to see Magda Zweck sitting alone. For some reason he found her presence comforting, even though, at root, he felt they had rather little in common. Her "damn the torpedoes" optimism wore most people down, but T thought it a small tax to pay for the amiable company of someone who actually took an interest in him. She had been the only faculty member to attend Olivia's funeral. T had never forgotten that act of grace.

"Oh, T!" sang Magda, brightly, as he took a seat next to her. "I'm so glad to see you. Are you excited about Nan's presentation?"

T smiled. "Not as excited as I was for the president's announcement."

Magda retained her own smile, but her expression was also pleading as if she wanted T to go on. But he simply patted her hand. "I'm happy to see you too."

There were only about ten other faculty members present. T could have easily been one of the "ghosts," and no one would have said a thing. Instead, here he was, waiting for Nan Hays to help him find lost portions of his brain.

"It's a fascinating topic," gushed Magda. "I often try to get my students to see things in a different light, understand things in new ways."

"Yes," nodded T, taking pains not to sound dismissive, "but that's different from turning on so-called unused portions of the brain like a light switch."

Magda, still smiling, regarded him charitably. "T," she said, a finger to her chin, "I'll bet you use the right side, the creative side, of your brain more than your analytical left side when you teach."

T sighed. "Magda, I use what I have."

There was a pattering of applause as Nan Hays stepped up to the lectern. T regarded her as one of those people whose entire countenance would be transformed for the better if she would just smile. She was a stern, fast-talking, no-nonsense go-getter who consistently taught overloads and served on a dizzying number of committees. T wondered when she had time to breathe. He had nothing against overworking, even though he had long ago honed his job down to a manageable size; but he didn't understand overworking and then complaining about it.

"I'm sorry I'm late," said Nan in a chop-chop manner as she brushed her bobbed gray hair from her face. This served only to reveal her weathered, blanched, rather severe features. "I was with the curriculum committee and we had old business as well as new business, so we went overtime. And after I'm done here it's on to the facilities and library committees. The work never ends. It just never ends. And then I have a double teaching overload this semester."

She delivered all of this intelligence while looking down and shuffling her papers. "Now," she finally said, "the brain."

T taught brain anatomy as part of his Human Biology course, so he felt immediately on the defensive when Nan, without so much as a nod to the structure of the organ, launched into a full-throated set of assertions about mysterious cerebral recesses—she called them "vesicles"—that modern living had suppressed but which could be "liberated" if one just learned the appropriate techniques. To this end, and coincidentally, Nan had written a new book—that she held up—titled *Holistic Approaches to Brain Function*, that she was willing to offer to her colleagues, for a short time only, at a forty percent discount.

My God, my God, thought T as he looked on in disbelief. His great fear was that Nan was going to refer to "Gestalts," a word he particularly despised.

"What I am trying to show is that I have discovered a new *Gestalt* for understanding not only the student brain, but the faculty brain as well."

There was no escaping the two-brain theory. If he got up now, he would draw attention to himself and run the risk of being accused of intolerance toward other viewpoints. So he sat, and stewed, and brooded. He occasionally stole a glance at Magda, who was leaning forward in her seat, kneading her hands, her eyes moist with hope for a better future through brain liberation.

About fifteen minutes into her talk, the theme took a curious turn. As if in league with the president's recent address, Nan Hays segued into a soliloquy about certain cryptic brain areas which she referred to as "minefields" capable of eliciting painful student emotions. "To this end," she said, "we pedagogues must take utmost care not to tread on areas that some students might find uncomfortable."

T found himself wondering if some sort of conspiracy were afoot. Since when were students deemed too fragile to confront difficult or challenging topics? When Nan was finished, she was given heartfelt applause. T couldn't bring himself to join in. He would have felt like an absolute hypocrite. He couldn't help noticing that Praveen had also remained unresponsive.

"How about a cup of coffee?"

"Excuse me?"

"Coffee," said Magda. "It will give us a chance to catch up."

"Oh. Yes, sure."

The two retreated to the faculty lounge, which was mercifully empty. The only other warm body was a female student worker, who moved quietly about her business, shadowlike. The two sat in a far corner by the large windows that looked out over the campus ash grove, just now tinged with the yellow of autumn. T didn't want to be asked what he thought of Nan's talk. However, Magda was more than willing to take up the slack. "Wasn't it great?" she said, scrunching her shoulders together.

T stared down into his coffee, stirring it in hypnotic fashion, studying the vortex he was creating. "Magda," he said, looking up, "of all my colleagues, you are most dear to me."

She melted. "What a nice thing to say. You mean a lot to me too. You should hear the things the students say about you."

T knew what students said about him. He read their comments on the teacher evals at the end of every semester. He was also a recipient of that *Students' Choice* teaching award. Still, it was nice to be acknowledged by a colleague. He went on. "Magda, I'm a scientist. I deal with conclusions based on evidence. Sometimes my investigations daunt my assumptions and I'm forced to change my mind."

Magda was looking at him with those deep blue, pleading eyes, as if she expected him to cry. But T was nowhere near tears. He was as dispassionate describing his approach to science as he was when actually doing it. "Nan's talk was not science. It was the expression of a desire to see the world work in a way that accords with her personal philosophy."

Magda was now looking through him, as if trying to focus on something in the distance behind his back. T realized that this was his problem. He had always had difficulty talking about subjects about which he had strong sentiments. Now was his chance to right that ship and speak plainly, if not to the forgiving Magda, then to whom?

"Magda, Nan was talking about her feelings. It wasn't science. It was no different than alchemy or astrology. They sound scientific, but neither is valid. I just can't buy into her mumbo-jumbo." The student moved past their table, carrying a load of dishes. Magda smiled up at her and then, incongruously, returned to T with, "She has a Ph.D."

T slowly shook his head. "You make having a Ph.D. sound like an excuse. It's not a guarantee of veracity. People with Ph.D.s can also be wrong. They can also be ignorant." T smiled. "Remember what the Wizard of Oz said to the scarecrow when he asked for a brain? Something about people at universities with no more brains than he."

Magda firmed her lip. "You sound critical of your own profession."

T took a sip of his coffee, already growing cool. "What's wrong with that? If we want academia to live up to its principles, we should be critical." He could see that he was not winning Magda over. She couldn't take her gaze from him, as if he were one of her clients who needed to be buoyed up. "Magda," he continued, "I'm not saying that teaching at a college isn't a great gig. It is. It's a fantastic gig. No time clock to punch, no one asking me where I'm going or when I'll be back. Plenty of time off, interesting students and colleagues, a library brimming with lovely books. But it's also highly artificial. I mean, the president's new policy requiring that we filter our syllabi through the provost so that so-called controversial material can be flagged. And now Nan Hays and her cockamamie theory about the brain being trip-wired to react to information that students might find disturbing. It's like she's riding shotgun on the president's runaway wagon."

Perhaps he had said too much. Magda's eyes had filled with woe. He held out an olive branch. "Maybe it's me," he said by way of conciliation. "People like Praveen and I don't seem to fit in anymore. We were the only two who didn't applaud Nan's talk. If I had thought there was even marginal truth in what she said, I would have given her some support. But, forgive me, Magda, I can't."

"What are you afraid of?"

The question belied Magda's skill in listening to people and then getting straight to what she saw as the point. In this case, she was pretty close to the mark.

T lowered his voice, even though, except for that student employee, they were alone. "Magda, it's not really fear, but more like an unease. That I'm going to say or do something—and not something that I haven't said or done before—that is going to elicit blowback in this new environment of...what's the word I'm looking for?" And then it struck him. "Intolerance."

Magda tilted her head to the side. "Do you think I'm intolerant?"

T sat back and regarded her at arm's length. "This has nothing to do with you. You're the most tolerant person I know. But I'm wondering if that's not part of the problem. I mean, must everything be tolerated?"

"What, in your opinion, shouldn't be tolerated?

"For a start? Aggression masquerading as righteousness."

SEVEN

T walked into his Introductory Biology lecture. Most of his twenty-five students had preceded him, but all of them were quietly communing with their devices. This silence, T knew, was a product of the technology. He was old enough to remember what teaching was like before smart phones. When he entered the classroom the students would be amiably chattering, happy to see one another, grooming their new friendships. His first task in those days—not so very long ago—had been to get them to quiet down and pay attention so he could begin the lecture. Oh, how he missed that opening moment, the good-natured jesting on his part about what on earth could be done with people who had so much to say and would prefer listening to each other rather than to him. But now it was like walking into a graveyard. T looked at this as his challenge to wake them up, engage them. But first, he had to disengage them from their devices.

T turned to the whiteboard and examined its slick, immaculate surface. The school had removed all the true—what were they, slate?—blackboards five years ago and had replaced them with the—what were they, vinyl?—dry erase variety. The reason, they said, was chalk dust, which got into the works of the computers. But T didn't like the dry erase markers and the asphyxiating stink of their volatile solvents. However, this was the new tool that had been given him, so he pressed on, uncapped the marker, got a whiff of the toxin, and wrote the word "GENE" on the board. Then he called the class to order, which didn't require much volume in light of the abject silence in the room.

The students stole their last, furtive glances at their phones as they reluctantly packed them away. The faculty was not of a mind about phones in class. Some didn't care and just taught around the texting masses. At the other extreme were those who were aggressively punitive, which T thought was also wrong-headed. Drawing a battle line between teacher and student was not a winning strategy: if the students joined forces, the instructor would never stand a chance. So T chose a sort of middle ground, making himself clear on the subject of phones, but with a light touch. "Please don't text while I'm teaching," he told them, with a twinkle in his eye, on the first day of each semester. "If I catch you texting you must immediately call your parents and tell them that you love them." This is all it took to warm his charges to the cause, after which he was able to explain, "Here's the deal. If you don't text while I'm teaching, I promise not to text when you come to me with a question or concern."

There was always this middle ground, then, in dealing with students, especially so-called "non-traditional" students with their galaxies of personal issues that required myriad "accommodations." This one needed more time on tests; that one a separate, quiet space; another an emotional support animal; and the capper: a recent student, an older woman, who had required (1) a special chair, (2) a note-taker, (3) a test reader, (4) double-time to complete tests, (5) her support dalmatian, and (6) all handout printed on yellow paper. This had brought T to muse that maybe the college could simply appoint a proxy for this student so she wouldn't have to come to school at all. He didn't confide this errant thought to Magda, for fear of being labeled a cynic.

T warmed to his genetics lecture. He loved the subject, which allowed him to reference all sorts of current, cutting-edge material, from viral variants to "designer" babies to cloning. There were those biologists who were rabid reductionists: to them the only thing that mattered was that particle of heredity known as the gene. T wasn't quite on board with them—life was too complex and multifaceted to be simplistic about it—but he did place due importance on those fragments of DNA shared by all living things, from mites to mushrooms to humans. "The DNA of chimpanzees and humans is ninety-nine percent identical," he lectured as the class scribbled away. "That one percent difference accounts for human language, art, science, and our enviable ability to dream forward in time."

T paused, allowing that thought to sink in. He walked away from the board and ambled among the desks. "Each of you is a unique collection of genetic information. Thirty billion humans have lived on earth since our species evolved, and there has never been anyone like you. Even if you have an identical twin, you will grow genetically different over time." He was standing in their midst now, like the mainmast on a sailing ship on which they were all passengers. He looked about, his eyes settling on each of them. And then, inspired, he quoted the poet Mary Oliver: "'What will you do with your one wild and precious life?'"

This is what the students liked about him. It was T's ability to warm to them, to make them feel that they mattered. He encouraged them because he knew that everyone needed to be encouraged. Most student crises—the self-doubt, the lack of organization, the homesickness, the feelings of stress—could be assuaged by quiet, caring words. "You're doing better than you think." "You're not one of the students I'm worried about." "If a person of your talent fails, how will everyone else do?" "You're unhappy in your major? Then change it." "You're unhappy being in school? Then leave. We'll be here if and when you decide to come back."

T returned to the board and pounded it just below the word GENE. "Before 1909 the word didn't exist. Gregor Mendel himself, the father of genetics, referred to what he called 'factors' as the units of heredity." T hung his head and chuckled. Then he looked up. "It's one of the great ironies in all of science history—that the laws of sex were discovered by a monk."

The class chortled amicably. This was T's stock in trade: kindling a light, welcoming, humorous, yet content-driven spirit in his classes. He knew that he had the lecture well in hand and that the students were following in his wake. Ideas began to flood his mind. Which way to go now? There were so many paths, so many interesting anecdotes to get his point across. Mendel had flunked out of college. The students needed to know that. In the old days, some people thought that if you took an ax to bed when you made love you would beget a boy. If a woman craves sweets, she's going to have a girl. This was the atmosphere Mendel was up against: there were no laws governing sex, in either plants or animals. It was, in the eyes of the Church, all God-ordained, so hands off. But Mendel had plowed right in, assuming that there must be laws that govern reproduction. "He performed thousands upon thousands of crosses on pea plants," T told his class. "He took a mathematical approach. After years of work, he presented his findings to the local natural science society. Their response?—Silence."

The students looked up as T allowed that last word to hover. Then, bringing a finger to his lips in a hushing gesture, he reiterated it in a whisper. "Silence." He walked back to the board and withdrew into himself, bringing his fingertips together and examining them. "I think that Mendel must have been broken-hearted. I once saw a dramatization in which the character playing Mendel remarks, 'Maybe I should have been cultivating piety instead of peas.'" T looked up as if snapping out of it. "Years after his death his work was rediscovered, at the turn of the twentieth century, and science has never been the same. Sometimes I think that, if there's only one word you need to take from this course, it's 'gene.'"

The students wrote the word down again.

And then, this: "As far as nature is concerned, the only reason each of us, or any living thing, exists, is to pass our precious genes to the next generation, after which we are, like salmon, disposable, like spent cartridges. Of course, as humans, we also have other reasons to live, which is what makes the human condition unique in the living world."

The period ended. The students applauded, closed their notebooks, and seized their phones to see what they had missed during the biology interregnum. They filed out, but one young man remained behind, still sitting at his desk in his long, black, hooded woolen coat. His gaze was fixed on T, who turned to him. “Do you have a question? What’s your name again?”

The student didn’t say a word. Still gazing at T, his expression blank, he slowly got up, gathered his things, and left the classroom.

Curious. T shrugged and gathered his things as well. He shut off the light, closed the door, and moved on to his next labor.

EIGHT

"Hey, Russki."

T stopped in mid-stride on the way to his office. He turned and saw Clive Gridley ambling up from behind. "Please don't call me 'Russki.' You know I don't care for it."

Clive wasn't capable of communicating without physical contact, so he clamped a beefy hand around T's upper arm. "C'mon, T, can't you take a little kidding? I mean, it's just between you and me. It's not like I announced it on the evening news."

In truth, T wasn't really offended by Clive's repeated jibe. He had learned not to expect more of the man. At some level, he felt sorry for him. He was loud and brash and self-righteous, and for all of these reasons, most of the faculty gave him a wide berth. He must have been aware of their aversion, but it only whetted his liabilities, making him louder and brasher at every opportunity. T knew enough basic psychology to peg his colleague as a lonely man striving for attention. He did have one useful strength, though: he was a vocal member of the faculty senate and a union representative. As such, he was vociferous in his advocacy for the teaching ranks, especially the overworked and underappreciated adjuncts, who worked without benefits or, for that matter, decent pay. T mustered a greeting, which was all it took for Clive to release his arm. "What's the news, Clive?"

T's inquiry electrified the jocular political scientist with the Santa Claus smile. Clive loved talking about senate doings, especially where intrigue was concerned. "The gang is abuzz about the president's Marxist dictate."

"So I'm not alone." T thought "Marxist" was a bit much, but Clive's heart was in the right place.

Clive chuckled. "Of course not. But you've been voted most likely to speak up."

"Will it change anything?"

Clive shrugged good-naturedly. "Ever hear of H.L. Mencken?"

"Of course. A brilliant literary journalist way back. It's a shame he's not being taught today."

Clive clapped. "Bravo, T. You and I have more in common than you think. Mencken once wrote, 'When they say it's not about money, it's about money.'"

T pleaded ignorance.

Clive gave him a friendly chuck on the arm. "C'mon, T. Open your eyes. Warm bodies, man. The school's open admissions policy. Every head has a dollar sign on it, and if the head flunks out, the school loses the dollar."

T winced. "So you're saying that we can't afford to alienate a single student by addressing topics that might offend them?"

Clive put up his hands. "Not me, bud." He thumbed the sky. "It's the higher-ups. As I said, you and I have more in common than you think. We should have a drink sometime."

"I don't drink."

"Well, maybe you're not a Russki after all." Clive belly-laughed at his own cleverness. "When I was in law school…"

"Wait," said T, raising a hand. "You went to law school?"

"Surprise," said Clive, spreading his arms as if his next move were a bear hug. "Brace yourself. I even graduated. I aimed for Cs so the experience wouldn't be a stressful one. I knew that nobody would look at my grades after I graduated. They just want to see the diploma."

T took a closer look at his colleague. He had thought that he knew everything he needed to know about Clive, but this was a genuinely interesting nugget. "Did you ever practice?"

Clive waved him off. "I was going to, but then I saw this opening for a poli-sci professor at our dear old school. I had just read a book called *ProfScam*—about all the nonsense we get away with—and it seemed like an easier way to earn a living. I mean, that four-month paid summer vacation can't be beat." He winked.

T wondered what Magda would make of Clive's brand of cynicism.

Clive checked his watch. "Oops. Gotta go. So, everything is well in your classes, right?"

"We started the genetics section today."

"Oh yeah, that's real firm ground," said Clive, rolling his eyes. "About as safe as evolution. Wait till the provost gets hold of you."

"I'll keep my head down."

"You don't understand," said Clive, sobering. "He's talking to each of us in turn, starting with senior faculty."

"Maybe I should get a lawyer."

"Ha!" roared Clive, throwing his head back. "I know where you can find one cheap!"

T watched as Clive retreated, his heavy frame rocking on slightly bowed legs, his pants cuffs dragging under his heels. T would never have imagined the sentiment he now felt for Clive, however fleetingly.

Wonder.

NINE

T KNEW NOTHING ABOUT the provost, except that he was a fairly recent hire from some school in Alabama. No one at Skowhegan wanted the job, except for Clive, who had failed in his bid, so the college had gone fishing elsewhere. Clive, despite losing out, had been thrilled when someone from a red state was installed, but his ardor seemed to have cooled as of late. ("He's a little too pushy for my taste.") Lawrence Graveline had burst onto the scene like a Mack truck, issuing an email to the faculty promising to "clean house," "make things ship-shape," and "get Skowhegan moving again!"

The thing was, there was no collective faculty sentiment that the house was soiled, that the ship was not seaworthy, or that the institution was stuck in neutral. In short, the bed was not too hard, not too soft, but just right for most folks. However, there were always those few who thrilled to the prospect of a firm hand, a declamatory personality, and a no-nonsense approach to administration. Even Boats, who had whittled his obligations down to the bare minimum, roused himself at a faculty meeting to declare his full support for someone who promised to "Get things done." Of course, if that included ensuring that faculty actually taught their classes, he would find his time at sea severely curtailed.

As for Clive's dispatch about individual faculty meetings with the provost, he had been right on the mark. When T got back to his office an email was waiting for him. The subject line read simply, *Meeting*. T opened the message and read: *I'm meeting with all faculty one-on-one. Your slot is tomorrow at 3. My office. See you then. – L*

T bristled. Not even a "Dear Professor" salutation, an inquiry as to whether this would be a good time to meet or, for that matter, a friendly closing gloss. And was the provost, in signing his email "L," making light of T's moniker? The whole tone of the message was wrong, and T found himself preoccupied with it for the rest of the day. This preoccupation accompanied him to his empty house. Well, not quite empty. When he entered, Tootsie came running up to him. She sat on her haunches at his feet, looked up at him, and meowed pitifully. "What? No food?" inquired T as he put his briefcase down and lifted the feline into his arms, where she purred contentedly. He walked into the kitchen and noted that Tootsie's bowl was still half full. He put her down, but she leaped back up into his arms. "Okay," he said, massaging the two sensitive nooks behind her ears, smiling as she squinted in ecstasy. "I'll work around you."

T opened the fridge and rummaged until he excavated the leftover pasta from the previous night. He nuked it in the microwave and, finally disengaging from Tootsie, sat down at the counter and slowly ate. The house was not big—only two small bedrooms—but it now felt cavernous. Something about the acoustics. Even padding about in his socks, every footfall seemed to resonate. A burglar would never have a chance of going undetected. Even when Tootsie was on the move, T knew exactly where she was. A mouse had ample warning and nothing to fear.

After eating, T moved to the good chair in the living room, with Tootsie nestled in his lap. Three of the walls were covered with books. Overflowing with books. Was it time to start culling? Keep only the ones that had become old friends? Did he really need all of Jean Auel's titles about the genius of prehistoric humans? Or his vegetarian cookbooks? All of that information could be garnered from the web. Let somebody else store it.

Oh, how he missed reading aloud. He and Olivia had spent many a night cuddled by the woodstove, books in hand. He felt that he had something of a tin ear for poetry, but when Olivia read it aloud it suddenly made sense. She had a knack for phrasing, for emphasizing particularly trenchant passages, after which she would raise her eyes from the text and glance at T, to make sure he had gotten the import. Did anyone still read poetry? He made occasional allusions to it in his biology lectures, but the students, perhaps because they thought well of him, only smiled. He once asked if any of them read poetry for pleasure. No one said a word.

Silence. That was the thing about Olivia. Her capacity for silence. Even when they had first met, she wasn't like most of the other women he had known—chattering as a means of calming their dating anxieties. On their first date, he and Olivia had taken a walk together in the woods surrounding the campus. He didn't recall their having exchanged a single word. And yet, when they came out at the other end of the path, he felt that he had learned a lot about her.

There was something in him that wanted to dwell upon that thought, but the provost—damnably—kept interceding. What right did he have to interrupt T's idyll, his pleasant memories of the loving relationship he had known? This thought pursued T through the long night until, very late, the blessed boon of sleep arrived.

TEN

THE ANTEROOM TO THE provost's office was occupied by his administrative assistant. Peg Hartford was a pleasant but long-suffering woman with a wearied look that conveyed the impression that she was beset by some ongoing tragedy. T therefore handled her carefully. He greeted her brightly. "Hi, Peg. Long time no see. I hope you're well. How's Errol?"

She looked up at T, standing before her desk, and smiled the painful smile of someone who has just been offered condolences upon the death of a loved one. Peg was a very private, very old-fashioned woman. She had her hair permed by her hairdresser daughter once a month and called her plumber husband at twelve every day to check in. She had been outside the state of Maine only once, years ago. A weekend in Cape Cod. "That was enough for me," she once confided to T at a Welcome Back breakfast.

"Oh, pretty good," she said. "He's got his work."

"How's the new provost?"

T noted Peg's hesitation. She adjusted the pencils in the wicker holder on her desk. "Oh, everything's running okay."

"I have a three o'clock appointment with him."

Peg glanced up at the clock on the wall. "Well, it's two fifty-eight, so I guess you got a coupla' minutes. He's a stickler for punctuality. He don't like neither early nor late."

T smiled. "What shall we talk about to kill two minutes?"

"Oh, I don't know," said Peg, amiably. "The garden's still producing."

Peg's Maine accent, with its broad a's, cheered T. It was so classic that it should have been bronzed. "Someone told me that you get tomatoes into December."

Her smile was more genuine now. "Oh, we'll be cannin' into the New Year, I s'pose. Errol loves his t'matoes."

Both were seventy and had been married for fifty-two years. T had been only thirteen when they had tied the knot. Being in Peg's presence made him feel young. "There you go," she said. "Three o'clock. I s'pose you can go on in. He don't like nobody bein' late."

T walked through the door into a rather long, narrow office with high ceilings. A long maroon runner led to a desk fronting the far wall, behind which the provost sat, his head down, scribbling away. "I'm here," announced T.

No response. The provost continued to scribble. T didn't like rudeness in a man. It had been drummed out of him by his father early on every time he failed to say "Thank you" for some grace. T decided to take control of the situation. He walked the runner and sat down in a chair in front of the desk. Still no response. T reached into his bag and pulled out Darwin's *The Voyage of the Beagle*. He began to read. This went on for five long minutes, at the end of which the provost looked up. "So you're...let me see here, I've written it down... How do you pronounce this? Tymo..."

Without taking his eyes from his book, T put up a hand. "Give me a moment. I'm almost at the end of my paragraph. I'll be right with you."

T was surprised at his own cheek. But he had stepped in it, determined now to put his full weight down. When he finally closed his book and looked up, the provost was staring daggers at him. His face was red, complementing his ring of rust-red hair circling a broad bald spot, his head nested in hunched shoulders. T noted his split nose. "Do you think I have all day?" he rasped.

T sensed that he had the advantage as long as he maintained his calm. "No, I don't. In fact, I've heard that you put a lot of emphasis on punctuality, as do I. It's an admirable trait. That's why I walked in at precisely three o'clock. That's the time you wanted to see me, wasn't it?"

Lawrence Graveline ran the back of his hand across his mouth as if removing a bad taste. He sat back in his swivel chair. He looked small. Raising both hands, he began to feather the air with his fingers, insect-like. T the biologist was fascinated. Then the provost leaned forward and launched his first volley. "What kind of business would you say this is?"

T didn't grasp the provost's meaning. "What business are you referring to?"

"This. The college."

"I've never thought of it as a business. Isn't it more of a service?"

The provost sat back again. He drew a finger to his lips and studied T. "I've heard about you."

T struck his own studious pose. "Oh? What have you heard?" T hated passive-aggressive interactions, these sideways conversations, the innuendo, and indirectness. But he felt he had waded into a swiftly-running stream and was being swept away.

"I've reviewed your file. The students seem to like you. And there's mention of a teaching award here. You're also a writer. *The New Yorker*? Very commendable."

T didn't say anything. He continued to look blankly at the provost, waiting for the other shoe to drop. This seemed to unnerve the man, who looked about as if taken off guard by T's lack of response. He finally alit on what was apparently his theme. "You're not the first faculty member I've spoken to. But you are the first who has not submitted his syllabus for my review."

T didn't understand. "My syllabi are on file for public access, Provost. You can see them any time you want."

The provost rocked his head. "God knows how old these 'on file' syllabi are. I need a current document from you, with all updates and edits."

"I'd be happy to email a copy to you." And then, after a pause, "Is that why you called me here?"

Lawrence Graveline darkened. "We've had a complaint," he said.

"A complaint?"

"From a student."

T readjusted his position in his chair and drew a hand to his chin. "About what?"

"Don't you know?"

"I have no idea."

"You teach biology?"

"I do."

The provost opened a manila folder, put on brown, horn-rimmed glasses, and scanned a document. "Did you tell your class, er, Introductory Biology, that the only reason we are here is to pass our genes on to the next generation?" The man looked up with accusing eyes.

T was more amused than discomfited by the so-called complaint. "I'll tell you precisely what I said. I said, 'As far as nature is concerned, the only reason any living thing exists is to pass its precious genes to the next generation'."

The provost was nonplussed. "Did you compare humans to salmon?"

"I did."

"Do you not think humans are a special case?"

"In some ways, yes, and I said as much. I said something to the effect that as humans we have other reasons to live as well."

The provost plowed on. "Did you compare humans to spent cartridges?"

T had had enough. "I'm uncomfortable being cross-examined."

The provost struck again. "You don't seem to know how the academy works."

T was primed, and he fired. "And you seem to know nothing about history, Provost. Attempts to intimidate teachers don't generally go well." Even as a child, T had never fought back. This was a new experience.

The provost tried a different tack. He struck a conciliatory tone. "I don't want to be your enemy."

T was having none of it. "Then what is it that you want?"

Lawrence Graveline closed the manila folder and folded his hands on the desk. "The same thing I've told other faculty. To be blunt..."

"Yes, please be blunt." T caught himself. Interrupting the man wouldn't help his cause, whatever his cause was.

Lawrence Graveline narrowed his eyes. "If you would let me finish. As per the president, I've directed the other faculty, your colleagues, to issue trigger warnings at every turn. This is why I asked to see your syllabi, so I could help you with this task."

T felt his ire rising as he struggled to maintain focus, control. "Provost, I don't know much about you. I don't even know what your field is. What is your field?"

"Well, my degree is in Hospitality Management."

T suppressed an impulse to smile. He almost didn't know in which direction to proceed with this objectionable man, but a choice had to be made. "And what do you know about biology?"

The provost shrugged. "Enough. I certainly know where the red flags are."

"Do you? What would be the red flags? Evolution? Taxonomy? Genetics? Molecular biology?"

He shrugged again. "All of the above. And no doubt more. Have I made myself clear?"

T moistened his lips. "I'm curious. How have my colleagues reacted to your directive?"

The provost smiled and brought up his hands. "They are all on board. They're part of the team and are acting in the students', and the college's, best interest." A pause. The two men regarded one another. "So what will it be?"

T knew exactly where he stood and what he wanted to say, what needed to be said. "Provost, I have been teaching biology at this school for almost forty years. These students are adults. I encourage open discussion of challenging topics in my classes."

The provost held up a finger. "With trigger warnings."

T raised his own digit. "Without trigger warnings."

The provost got to his feet and turned his back to T. He looked out the window onto the campus green, his hands resting on the small of his back. "I also want you to apologize to this student."

"Excuse me?"

"You're to apologize to the aggrieved student."

"For what?"

"For discomfiting him. For upsetting him." He turned about and faced T, bringing an index finger to his temple. "For messing with his brain."

"How do you know all these things to be true?"

The provost threw out an accusing finger. "I've had it with you," he growled. "You have your orders. Number one, trigger warnings, and number two, apologize to this student. His name is Bradley Maun. He has a very specific reason for being upset."

T got up and straightened himself out. "Provost, with all due respect, you're making it sound as if I intentionally targeted this student."

Lawrence Graveline, still standing, nodded aggressively. "You did, Professor Tar... Tarna..."

"Tarnaszewski."

"You don't seem to understand how the adolescent brain, with its hidden recesses, operates."

T bridled at the accusation. "Provost. Mr. Graveline. I have never, and will never, target a student in any way. But I will talk with this student, to see where exactly the difficulty lies, because I feel that you've been less than candid with me. I think you know more than you're saying."

Lawrence Graveline was growing redder by the moment as if approaching a bursting point. "There is such a thing as insubordination."

"This isn't the military."

The provost had only three concluding words: "We shall see."

T left his office, pausing only momentarily to take his leave of Peg Hartford, who looked even more pained now that she had no doubt eavesdropped on their conversation. T exited the building, marched past the student union, past the library, and past the chemistry building before telling himself to slow down, take a breath. In giving himself that pause, he allowed an echo of his meeting to come to the fore. Those references to the brain. They sounded all too familiar.

ELEVEN

T felt a need to call Magda Zweck. When she picked up the phone he almost didn't know where to begin. "I think it's best if we meet in person," she said. "It will also give you a chance to get your thoughts in a straight line."

T realized that she was right, although he wasn't comfortable being handled like a client. "Magda," he said, "right now I need a friend. Promise you'll listen to me before saying anything."

"That's the least you can expect. Of course I'll listen. The weather is still nice. Let's sit outside in the ornamental garden. Are you free at two?"

"Yes. I'll see you there. Thanks."

T was convinced that this was the right move. He wanted to talk to this Bradley Maun, but not quite yet. He had long ago learned not to be reactive about these things. A day's delay had a way of putting things in perspective. On rare occasions, he received an angry email from one of the students in his online Biology of Cancer class. They didn't know him, had no sense of his personality, and did not have the benefit of in-person, after-class chats. All they saw at their end was a grade they deemed unjust. The response? A damning email launched like a torpedo. T's answer to such emails was always the same: "Do me a favor. Think about what you wrote here, and send me another message tomorrow. I'll answer you in detail then." Invariably, the student's follow-up email was conciliatory if not apologetic, creating the space necessary for understanding to begin. In the same vein, if Bradley Maun was on the warpath, it could only help matters to allow him time to gather his thoughts, allow his ire to ebb. All would then be well.

These were the thoughts that occupied T as he arrived on campus, parked, worked for a while in his office, and then, towards two, made his way to the ornamental garden at the edge of campus. The spot was an oasis of calm and beauty, its umbilicus a graceful white gazebo set down in its center like a gem in a crown. It was a shame it was so little visited by students, faculty, or staff. This is where he found Magda, seated on one of the benches in the gazebo, her eyes closed and chin up, relishing the still-warm sun. T paused and regarded her. If he had never connected with Olivia, might Magda have been…?

"T." Her eyes open now, she smiled at him. "Isn't this a beautiful day?"

He entered the gazebo and sat down at the opposite end of the bench. He looked out at the trees and shrubbery, slowly shedding their red, orange, and yellow leaves with every gust of the breeze. "On a day like this it's easy to understand why there are so many poems about autumn but few, if any, about summer. Change is more relevant to the human condition than stasis."

Magda pressed a hand to her chest. "T, that's lovely."

He struck a faux pose of triumph. "That's because I'm a lovely man."

"Even lovely men need friends."

T nodded. "Yes, that's why I asked to see you. I had my sit-down with the provost. Have you had an opportunity to meet the man yet?"

Magda shook her head. "No. But how did it go?"

"I won't mince words. Not well. He seems to be one of those people who look to the military for his organizational model."

"What was the issue that required a military solution?"

T sighed. "Magda, one of my students objected to something I said in class. The provost chastised me for not running my syllabus by his desk, even though it's available online. No matter, I'm happy—well, not happy, but you know what I mean—I'm happy to send him a copy, but he also demanded that I apologize to the student."

Magda waved a hand. "Wait. Back up. Give me some context

here. What exactly did you say that set the student off?"

"We're doing the section on genetics. I said that living things are primarily driven to pass on their genes to their offspring. I also added a gloss about humans, saying that our species has other reasons to persist as well."

Magda hummed and looked into the distance. Then she returned to T. "And how did the student react?"

"If I'm correct about who the student was, he must have been the one who was last to leave the classroom. He glanced at me, and I asked if he had any questions. He didn't say a thing, just left the room. Then I went to my office."

"And you think it was what you said about genes?"

T threw up his hands. "That's what the provost inferred."

Magda shrugged. "Have you spoken with the student yet? It seems to me that that's the place to start, right?"

This was self-evident to T. After all his years of teaching he had interacted with countless students one-on-one and had resolved as many issues. But this time there was a particular feeling of dread in the air. He sat back and struck a wistful pose. "Bradley Maun."

Magda was blank. "That's the student? I don't know him. Maybe he's first year and hasn't crossed my radar yet."

T folded his hands. "You know, I've dealt with so much over forty years of teaching. Even the occasional belligerent student. But it was usually because of a grade, and I was always able to arrive at a reasonable resolution. Even if the student wasn't quite satisfied, they knew that I was taking them seriously and trying to be fair."

"So why is this different? Once you talk to the student this may all pass as well."

"I fully intend to. But at this point, it's not the student who concerns me. It's the provost's demand that I apologize and that I install those blasted trigger warnings. Since when did schools have political officers?"

Magda listened to his every word, her expression subdued. And then, a gesture. She reached up and touched the side of his head. "You've kept your color well," she said, studying his locks. "Only a bit of salt in the pepper. They say that's a sign that you've mostly avoided stress in your life."

"Magda…"

"Shh. There's a message here. Don't get sick over this. You know how to deal with students; you don't need me to tell you anything about that. As for the provost, it's not time to go to war with him. You're senior faculty, tried and true. He messes with that at his peril."

T took her hand and squeezed it. "Thank you, Magda. I do cherish you. But if worse comes to worst…?"

Magda clutched his hand in both of hers. "First things first. Talk to the student."

TWELVE

T EMAILED HIS INTRODUCTORY Biology and Biology of Cancer syllabi to the provost but without the requested trigger warnings. He was especially proud of the Introductory Biology syllabus as it stood. It was the emblem of a course with a solid track record of success. It filled every semester and had a waiting list to boot. Despite this, students often begged T to waive them into the course, above and beyond the room's capacity to accommodate them. Sometimes he gave in and the mendicant students had to sit in folding chairs by the door, taking notes on their laps. Is this the course the provost wanted to mess with?

T gathered his things and headed for class. On edge now, he knew he would have to confront Bradley Maun. But when he walked into the full classroom a couple of minutes before the start of the lecture, he immediately noted the one empty desk in the back. Perhaps Bradley Maun, in indignation, had dropped the course. This would certainly simplify things. But then T realized that it wasn't a question of one student and one thing that he, as the teacher, had said in class. There was a sea change afoot. Expectations and sensitivities were different, and a controlling provost was now at the helm. It was only a matter of time before T came to loggerheads with the new political environment. In this light, he found himself wishing that Bradley Maun was in class, so matters could be discussed here, now, and head-on.

Once the lecture commenced, T lost himself in the material. He described with great aplomb the beautiful work of Gregor Mendel, whose greatest boon had been flunking out of college. It had given him the time and space at his monastery to carry out years of solitary, focused work with pea plants, which ultimately led to his establishing the basic laws of heredity. As T pivoted between the white board and his students, though, he couldn't help stealing glances at that one empty desk and wondering where Bradley Maun might be at that moment. He couldn't help feeling that the vacant desk was a blemish on his course, given the high demand for seats. It was still early enough in the semester for a wait-listed student to join the class. If Bradley Maun intended to drop Introductory Biology, now was the time to act.

"Next time," said T as he laid the marker to rest on the ledge of the board, "we will look at the genetic cross that made Mendel's reputation, although, sadly, tragically, he wouldn't live to see his work vindicated."

The students applauded warmly. A couple lingered after class to ask for clarification on this or that point. Another approached T with a plea for an extension on a lab assignment, which he granted. He left the building and headed back to his office to tend to his other, online course. As he crossed the campus green he noted how quickly autumn was progressing. They were at peak color now, and the mornings were crisp but not yet frigid. It had been so mild only yesterday, but now he was pulling the collar of his jacket closed as he leaned into the stiff wind. And then, in the distance and off to his right, he noticed a figure standing alongside one of the maples. Tall and thin, T recognized him in his signature black hooded bench warmer, which was open and flapping in the wind. His button-down shirt was also untucked and blowing about, yielding glimpses of the boy's navel. The oversized hood was up and obscured some of his face. Reflecting the current fashion, his jeans were slashed at the knees. His bare feet were startlingly white against the still-green grass.

There was no avoiding him now. One of them had to be the adult here. T altered his trajectory and walked toward Bradley Maun, who didn't make the least movement. With his blank stare, the hands obscured by the long, black sleeves, the flapping coat, the bare feet, the frozen aspect, stringy dark hair blowing about his face, he could have passed for one of those ghostly figures erected on lawns at Halloween. How could a human being stand so stock-still?

When T was within ten paces, the student took a step back. "Bradley," said T, raising a hand in greeting, "we should talk."

Still blank, still staring, Bradley Maun backed off in tandem with T's movement toward him. T stopped, and so did he. T took another step, and Bradley Maun moved back one step.

T stood there, the frigid breeze stroking his face, and looked at his student. "Now isn't this ridiculous? The provost told me you had a complaint about class. I'm your teacher. Let's talk it out."

In a choreographed fashion, Bradley Maun extended one leg and slowly, deliberately, pivoted around, military fashion, until his back was to T. Then he marched off, with T looking after him. He never turned again, never said a word. T watched as he receded into the distance and, eventually, disappeared down a walkway between the gym and the business building.

It didn't compute. This silent apparition just didn't seem like someone who could animate himself to the point of running to the provost to voice a complaint. And if he had, and was anticipating an apology, why was he skittering now?

THIRTEEN

T WAS CHAGRINED THAT he again found himself turning to Magda.

"That's what I'm here for."

T winced. She made it sound like some kind of service, and that he was one of the customers. But he thought too much of her to voice this, at least in so many words.

"Magda, I don't want this situation to color our relationship. I just need to know that I'm not overreacting or letting it get to me. But there's been a development." All of this was over the phone, while T sat in his office, gazing out the window.

"I'm listening."

He went on to tell her about the odd interaction—or lack of it—with Bradly Maun on the college green.

Magda hummed.

"And he wasn't in class today," continued T. "Even if I had intended to apologize, there wouldn't have been an opportunity."

Magda hummed again. "As I said, I don't know this student, but I'm wondering if Nan Hays does. She's a licensed clinician and works with a small number of students. They're the ones whose needs go beyond what I can offer as a counselor."

The mention of Nan Hays gave T pause.

"T? Are you still there? Hello?"

He moistened his lips and refocused on the conversation. "Yes. I'm sorry. Got distracted. Yes, I'll talk to Nan. I just hope she didn't notice that I didn't clap at the end of her brain talk."

"Nan's all business," said Magda. "Just stick to the facts and don't even mention your feelings. Also, don't try to interpret Bradley's motives. This is good advice. I deal with Nan all the time."

"And…?"

"T, I know you well enough to confide that she and I are not what you would call friends, but our relationship is cordial. She has a powerful personality and a need to be the alpha."

"I see. The bride at every wedding and the corpse at every funeral."

Magda laughed. "Yes. Bear that in mind and use it to your advantage. By the way, have you had any more contact with the provost?"

"No. All's quiet on the western front. But he doesn't seem like the kind of person to let things go. I sent him my syllabi and assume he's going through them with a fine-tooth comb, looking for red flags. Or maybe he just had a stroke when he read them." T could share these jibes only with Magda.

"T, I just have to think that this too will pass. I mean, how much time is the provost going to devote to the strange case of T and the perturbed student?"

There it was again, that perpetual, impulsive optimism that sometimes drove the realist in him to distraction. But the underlying chemistry of their relationship also served to dilute his impulse to push back against what he sometimes saw as naivete. "I'll talk to Nan."

"Good. And keep me posted?"

"Of course. Who else understands, or even cares?"

After hanging up, T sent off a genial email to Nan Hays, asking for a sit-down. He hadn't had many conversations with her over the years, exchanging mostly pleasantries at the Welcome Back breakfast or while waiting for a faculty meeting to begin. He had certainly never given her any reason to think ill of him, in light of his teaching reputation and all the praise heaped on him by his students.

T tended to his online cancer course for about an hour. This was the course designed to cater to those students who needed to work asynchronously due to the competing commitments in their lives. T would have preferred to teach the course live, but it was such a hit online—drawing students from all over the state—that the school had set it in stone just the way it was. It cost almost nothing to offer an online course, so Skowhegan College raked in a nice profit. T was reminded of the Mencken quote Clive Gridley had offered up. *When they say it's not about money…*

As if aware of his rhythms, Nan's email popped up on T's screen just as he was signing out of his course. The message was curt: *Yes, of course. How about today at three? My office?*

T fired back in kind. *I'll be there. Thanks.*

Nan's office was in one of the older, red-brick buildings that fronted the campus green. It hailed from some long-gone day when it had served as a regional public school, one of the first as one-room schoolhouses passed into history. T liked these old buildings and their attention to detail: the gracefully curved corbels supporting the eves, the filigreed stonework framing the front door, the high ceilings. Walking in, T immediately felt that it was the appropriate place for a psychologist to have her office. In his mind's eye, he could see Sigmund Freud emerging from one of the recesses, puffing on a cigar, on his way to conquer the world with his new way of seeing things.

T knocked and heard the call from within. He entered an expansive office—an embarrassingly large amount of space for one faculty member. Most of the teaching faculty had cramped quarters, but Nan enjoyed a casbah of luxury from which she could have fought off an invading army. Besides her classic oak desk—behind which she looked small and retreating—there was room for a sofa, bookcases, a couple of easy chairs, a refrigerator, an antique sideboard, and several oak filing cabinets. And there was still room to spare. T was surprised that there was no leather-upholstered analyst's couch in the mix. A magnificent, round Persian rug adorned the center of the room. It was so elegant that T was hesitant to walk on it. Should he remove his shoes? "Thank you for taking the time to meet with me, Nan," he called from the far edge of the rug. That seemed like the appropriate thing to say. He didn't want to feel too much like a mendicant.

Nan gestured toward him. "Well, why are you hovering? Step forward."

"What a beautiful floor treatment," said T as he slowly moved across the tight weave, feeling it give way with every step. He arrived at one of the leather easy chairs and sat down. He ran his fingers along the brass rivets on the armrests.

"You wouldn't believe how much a good Persian rug costs," Nan said as she shoved her work aside.

What a condescending thing to say. Of course he knew they were expensive. How presumptuous.

At that moment there was a knock. Nan looked disgusted. "Come in," she said, wearily, giving each syllable equal weight. T turned and saw a student, a young woman, sheepishly poke her head in the door. She looked vaguely familiar. "Oh," she said. "I didn't know you were busy." She looked rigidly at T, who smiled.

"Come back later, Irena," said Nan. "We'll talk then."

Once the student had disappeared, Nan returned to the moment. "Look at all this work," she said as she regarded several thick folders on her desk. "I just finished going through a pile of applications for the search for the new English prof, and now there's an opening on the curriculum committee I'll need to fill. It just never ends."

T managed a friendly tone. "Why don't you say no? God knows you do more than your share already."

Nan threw him an incredulous look. "Say no? If I say no, who will do the work? Will you?"

This was a game T had no intention of playing. "I admire your energy," he said.

Nan looked disgusted. "Thank God somebody does. I recall something President Shibbles said when he was at the helm here many years ago. He said, 'An institution is incapable of showing gratitude.'"

My God, thought T. *Is that what the job was about? Eliciting gratitude?* "I won't take up too much of your time," he said, intent on keeping the conversation on track. "I'm having a problem with a student and was wondering if you could help me in any way."

Nan's defenses were palpable. She put up a hand. "You need to know from the outset that I'm limited in what I can tell you."

"Confidentiality," breathed T.

"Yes," confirmed Nan. "So long as you understand this."

"I understand."

Nan folded her hands on the desk as if to keep them from doing more work. "Talk," she said.

"Bradley Maun."

At last, a crack. It was unmistakable. Something was working its way across Nan's face. "What else do you want to tell me?"

"He objected to something I said in class. He went to the provost. Then he was absent from class. I saw him on the green, but when I approached him he backed off and ran away." T hoped this dispassionate, machine-gun approach would appeal to Nan.

"Did he run or did he walk?"

"Does it matter?"

"I just want things to be crystal clear."

T smiled. "Nan, nothing is ever crystal clear. That's why I'm here. The provost directed me to apologize to him."

"Did you?"

T sat back and took a deep breath. "As I said, he retreated when I approached him."

The cross-examination continued. "Were you going to apologize?"

"No. But I did want to speak with him, to see what his concerns were."

Nan glanced at the clock on the wall. Then she turned to T. "What, in your opinion, seems to be bothering this student?"

In my opinion? "Nan, if the provost is being accurate, I know exactly what's bothering this student. Something I said in class while lecturing on genetics."

"What did you say?"

"Basically, that the primary reason for existence, for any organism, is to pass on its genes to the next generation."

Nan bobbed her head back and forth as if the concept were debatable. "And why did this student find that objectionable?"

T raised his hands. "That's why I'm here. I thought that maybe this Bradley Maun, if he is so deeply troubled, came to you."

Nan loaded for bear. "What do you mean, 'so deeply troubled'? Are you suggesting a diagnosis?"

This was absurd. "Of course not. But I think I'm qualified to say that something is bothering this student. Again, he complained to the provost."

Nan's fingers danced among the papers and folders on her desk as if offering a subliminal message that her time was rare and valuable. "I can tell you that Bradley Maun has made contact with me."

T exhaled audibly. All that work to get at such a simple answer. Nan went on. "The adolescent brain is a delicate organ," she said, incongruously. "It is complex and fragile."

T felt his blood pressure rising. What bullshit. He couldn't take it anymore. "Nan. Professor Hays. I teach the anatomy and physiology of the brain. These young students are tougher than we are. Their brains are no more delicate than ours. If anything, they're more resilient. Further, I would suggest that the brain grows more complex with age. Or would you say that, by extrapolation of your point, a baby's brain is more complex than an adult's?"

He had stepped into it now. He watched as Nan Hays threw herself back in her swivel chair. She normally looked weathered and weary, but T had succeeded in electrifying her. "Do you really want to debate the brain with me?" she charged, launching herself forward again and laying her hands on the desktop, steadying herself. T opened his mouth to answer, but she inserted a paragraph. "I saw you at my talk on accessing the hidden potential of the brain. It was a talk that was of benefit to both students and faculty. Did you notice how well received it was? Well, by most. I understand that you were dismissive of my so-called mumbo-jumbo. You likened it to astrology. Professor T, that's no way to treat a colleague. Do you think I didn't notice that you didn't clap?"

It was a few moments before T realized that his mouth was still open. He snapped it shut. Furious now, he labored to not say another word. Instead, he struggled up from the easy chair, nodded toward Nan Hays, turned, and retreated across the Persian rug. At the far end, he turned and cast a glance at her. "It's quite an office," he said and left.

He had never felt such anger toward a colleague before. He hoped only that he would be reasonably calm when he approached Magda to ask her why. Why the betrayal?

FOURTEEN

An email from Magda was waiting on T's computer. He didn't look at it. At the end of the day he went home, fed Tootsie, corrected a pile of student papers, and went to bed. He had anticipated a fitful sleep, but instead, he dreamed. For all he knew it wasn't a dream. Perhaps his father had really come to him, to comfort him and remind him that there once were happier days. His seven-year-old self appeared, holding his father's hand. They were standing by a railroad siding, admiring a red caboose. His father had loved trains and had communicated this love to his son. Little Tymoteusz glanced up at Papa. Already looking sick with his final illness that would, many years later, take him, his face was drawn and ashen, his body so very thin. He nonetheless mustered the strength not only to smile, but to reach down, take his son under his arms, and hoist him, with a great bellowing groan, into the air. He set him down on the rear platform of the caboose and watched as the train slowly chugged off, the father waving at his son, calling after him, "Have a good trip!" Tymoteusz waved back and continued to wave until his father became a mere pinpoint in the distance before vanishing entirely.

Something woke T. It wasn't the shock of the dream or the image of abandonment and aloneness it contained. Oddly, and coincidentally, it was the premonitory rumbling in the distance of the freight train that came through so infrequently now in this age of the demise of so many things. T lay in bed, wide awake now. The train blew its horn and the windowpanes rattled in the wooden frames of the old house. The locomotive was approaching the nearby crossing, but there was no way of telling how close it was. All T knew was that it was there, and it was on the move, a behemoth rumbling through at an ungodly hour. It was as if it were his duty to awaken to acknowledge the right of way of a superior force.

Sleep never returned. T lay awake listening to the creak of the clapboard house as the wind howled about the eves, a tree branch scratched against a window, an occasional car roared down the street. He was betwixt and between about the situation he found himself in. On the one hand, he was disappointed in himself for allowing something so trivial to preoccupy him. On the other hand, was it really so trivial? Forty years! A dedicated, compassionate teacher, an accomplished writer, a companionable colleague. Why now? Why should things be difficult now? Olivia had been the assertive one. Maybe there were indeed those who had had issues with him before but were fearful of tangling with his articulate, outspoken wife who had been so protective of him. Should he have allowed this? Since her death things were not as clear; he was less adept at reading the motivations of others. Maybe he was losing it. And then, like a train moving onto a switch track, his mind shifted. Magda. He would have to talk to, no, confront her. Now that he knew he couldn't confide in her he was again alone on that caboose, receding into the distance, en route to who knew where. He rolled over in bed, but sleep never returned.

T's mind was still racing when he finally rose from bed. He thought he would be exhausted from lack of rest, but he wasn't. He moved from bathroom to kitchen to Tootsie, mechanically addressing each task, utilizing muscle memory because his mind was elsewhere. Magda, the provost, Nan Hays, Bradley Maun. Were there really people who could shrug off such concerns? Maybe Ted Toth. Yes, maybe Boats had the right idea. The problem for T was that, since Olivia's death, his work had become his life. For Boats, it was simply the thing that kept him afloat.

When T got to his office he booted his laptop. Within moments the first volley of emails appeared on his screen. Fifty-two new messages on top of the seven hundred that were still in his Inbox. T thought back to the pre-email days. Did he ever receive fifty-two letters in a day? Did he ever have seven hundred pieces of mail lying on his desk? He managed a smile of silly disbelief when he considered how inconsequential most of the emails were. People actually took the time to sit down and type out these things.

Human Resources would like to remind you to play it safe this Halloween.

When you see one of our groundskeepers, thank them for keeping up with the fallen leaves.

Remind your students that the deadline for dropping a course without financial penalty is October 5.

This is Dental Hygiene Week.

T derived palpable pleasure from deleting these messages. In fact, the lettering on his "delete" key was all but worn away. And then, before his eyes, another email appeared.

Does the Provost have your syllabi?

It was from Peg. T wrote a measured reply to the kind but delicate administrative assistant, affirming that the syllabi had been sent a couple of days ago.

T continued to read through the messages. Buried in the mire was another from Magda. *You OK?*

His ire had by now receded to a low thrum of consternation. He didn't relish the approaching confrontation, but he knew it had to take place.

I'd like to talk. I have time after my lab section today. 1? My office or yours?

He liked the "my office or yours" gloss. It was a subtle signal that the meeting would smack of some level of formality. A few moments later the reply: *Yours will work.* He was happy for this, as it would give him the home-court advantage.

His only teaching obligation that morning was a lab for his Introductory Biology course. This gave him pause to wonder whether Bradley Maun would be absent from this class as well. If he was, it would be a stronger signal that he intended to drop the class. T considered that this might go a long way toward easing his mind and would perhaps allow him the emotional space to figure out what the issue had been, since no one had yet told him.

T fetched his binder and headed out of the building into a steadily warming day. The leaves were cascading in droves now, crunching underfoot. How the Maine fall quickened the blood! He felt himself already bracing for the winter to come. The *Old Farmer's Almanac* predicted a bitter affair.

"Jesus!" T spun about and there stood Clive Gridley, who had just administered a resonant slap on his back. "How about some warning next time? At my age, I'm in heart attack country."

Clive's Santa Claus smile was radiant, bunching his jowls up under his eyes. "Aw, Russki, it's just a friendly greeting."

If T were capable of such meanness, he would have replied, *I'm not your friend.* But instead, he registered an expectant gaze.

"So, the provost talk to you yet?"

"We had our chat."

"How did it go?"

T questioned how much he should divulge to the loquacious and indiscreet Clive. He decided to test the waters. "A bit difficult."

Clive threw him a sidelong glance. "C'mon," he said. "You can't kid a kidder. Look, I'll show you mine if you show me yours."

"Clive..."

The political scientist grew serious. "I had mine with him as well. He doesn't beat around the bush, does he? Told me he didn't like unions. My hearing sucks, so at first, I thought he said 'onions.' So I said, 'Neither do I,' and he perked up like we could be buddies or something. Like he was pleasantly surprised that the union rep was anti-union. But when I realized what he was really talking about, well, you can imagine the rise it got out of me. It ended on a really bad note." Clive lowered his voice. "You know what he said to me?

He said, 'I'm gonna wear you out, Slick.' He called me 'Slick'!"

T took heart from this confidence. So he wasn't the only one who seemed to have trodden the provost's bad side. "Did he address the issue of trigger warnings?"

"Oh, yes," said Clive as he glanced up at the clear blue autumn sky. "I just smiled pleasantly and moved the conversation elsewhere, to union matters, if only because this is what seemed to get under his skin. Why do you ask? Was that the sticking point with you?" Clive winced. "Don't tell me. Evolution."

T appreciated Clive's candor. "Not per se. I have an issue with a student. Or better said, the student has an issue with me."

"With *you*? You're the only one of us who gets an ovation after a lecture." And then, with a wave, "Well, we all have our share of difficult students. I had one who lodged a grievance because, out of the goodness of my heart, I brought some brownies to the final exam. I told the class there were walnuts in them. Can you see where this is headed? Right. One of the kids had a nut allergy and complained to the higher-ups that it was attempted murder. Once I explained to the honchos that I had forewarned the class about the walnuts, you can imagine how quickly that one wound up in Nowheresville. But I never brought goodies in again. It's not worth it. A real shame, 'cause I love brownies." As he said this he rolled a palm over his expansive gut.

T listened patiently to Clive's anecdote and found himself warming to the man, for his unselfconsciousness if nothing else. "My situation is a little more complicated than brownies, but I appreciate the commiseration."

Clive checked his watch. "Well, it'll work out. It always does. Let me know when you want to have that drink."

T continued on to his lab. When he got there, all of his students were already sitting at the benches—except for Bradley Maun. Was that it, then? The appropriate thing to do was send the student an email—cc'ing the registrar—asking if he was still in the class. In the meantime, T leaned into the material and soon had his students working on an exercise classifying fossils into the various geological periods. It was a quiet, contemplative exercise that didn't involve chemicals, computers, or complicated apparatus. The students began to work in their groups as T meandered about the room, occasionally looking over their shoulders, encouraging them, answering their questions. They were a good bunch and seemed to like each other. It was the type of activity where they could chatter happily about other things while doing their work. For T, this was the truly rewarding part of teaching—the Socratic, incidental interactions with individual students as questions arose; the opportunity for others to listen as he quietly explained a concept or raised questions of his own for a student to ponder. It was sweet.

The two-hour period flew by. "Make sure your specimens are put away and please get your worksheets in by the deadline. I hope you've noticed how beautiful the day is. Be good to yourselves and spend at least part of it outside." He smiled and they returned the sentiment as they filed out the door.

As T gathered his things he felt a sort of dread building as he contemplated his meeting with Magda. The more he tried to gather his thoughts the more elusive the task became. He decided to throw himself into the breach and hope for the best. It was in this frame of mind that he exited the building and headed for his office. He wanted to get there a few minutes before Magda, to tidy things up a bit. And then he reconsidered. *Why should I tidy anything up? This is my nest, take it or leave it. I'm not going to tidy anything up. Not even for Magda.*

All thoughts of straightening his space became moot when he approached his office and saw Magda hovering there, looking bright and pretty. When she caught sight of him she smiled. Her eyes sparkled with that light of recognition that she was looking at a friend.

T mustered a rather sick smile, which could not have been lost on the astute and perceptive Magda. Still, she retained her sunniness and opted for a pleasantry. "It was chilly out there this morning. Brrr."

T opened the door and walked in ahead of her. "Excuse the mess," he said, and immediately regretted even this minor relinquishing of his high ground.

"It's not a mess, T," countered Magda as she sat in a chair next to his cluttered desk. "It's the workspace of an active mind."

"It's very kind of you to say that," said T, still not looking directly at her.

Magda's smile slowly melted away. She patted her cowlicks and sighed. "I'm picking up some interesting vibes from you."

That was his opening. T looked sternly at her. "You should," he said, and as soon as he primed his thoughts with those two words, the dam broke. "How could you? How could you tell Nan Hays, of all people, what we had talked about in the faculty lounge? She was livid. She talked to me as if I were an inferior species. And she quoted me almost verbatim, even getting the 'mumbo-jumbo' part right. Magda, I felt mortified and betrayed. If I've lost you, who will I count on? Boats?"

T sat back. He considered how proud Olivia would have been of him for such a cogent synopsis of a pointed event. As for Magda, her face was frozen into a grim rictus. She was not looking at T; she was looking through him. He swallowed and ran a hand over his face. He watched as her lip began to quiver. *Oh, damn,* he thought. *Stay strong. Don't give in. It's her choice whether to cry or not.* And then, "Please don't cry." He recalled something Olivia had once said with a dismissive wave when T told her one of his female students had cried because she had gotten a C on a test. "T, women cry all the time."

Magda sniffed and pulled herself together. "That was a hell of a shot, T."

"Do you deny it?"

One more sniff and she was back in control. "Of course I do."

T sat up in his chair. "Didn't you hear anything I said? You're the only person I confided in, and it was like Nan was reading from a transcript."

Magda didn't answer immediately. T wished she would, so he could retain his momentum. He had never before noticed how audibly the clock on the wall ticked. Nor how, this time of day, the low sun pierced his office window, illuminating the space. "Magda," he said, "I'm just asking why."

She came alive. "No, you're not. You're drawing a conclusion.

You're being hurtful. You're accusing me of something I didn't do."

T threw up his hands. "We were alone. There were no listening devices that I was aware of. Do you see that I'm approaching this scientifically, looking at the evidence dispassionately?"

A light went on in Magda's eyes. "We weren't alone."

T slowly shook his head. "I don't see how…" And then he remembered. The student employee who had been there that day. But she was so distant, so busy about her work. *My God, I've seen her.* T swallowed, loud enough for Magda to hear. "Magda," softly now, "do you know who that student worker in the faculty lounge was, the day we were there?"

"Yes. She's in my Intro to Middle School Counseling class. Her name is Irena. She's very quiet but quite bright. Doesn't say much in class, but has good test grades." And then, "She could be one of Nan's protégés."

T looked away and gazed about as if scanning the floor for a lost paperclip. Without looking back at Magda, he murmured, "She's not quiet."

It was hard to keep Magda down. She brightened, as if this were a new nugget of interest, displacing T's misguided rhetoric. "I think you may have your answer. The question is, what do you do now, if anything?"

T looked at Magda again. "First things first. I apologize to you. I should have known better. I also know better than to blame Bradley Maun for my behavior. I'm a grown man and I'm responsible for my actions."

Magda smiled. "That's a good start. You're forgiven. What are you going to do next?"

T pressed his palms together and brought his hands to his lips. "I—I don't know, to tell you the truth. This Irena didn't do anything wrong per se. And it's unseemly to go after a student in any case. But Nan. Did she plant Irena in the lounge? No, she couldn't have. She had no way of knowing we would be there or what we might be talking about. So I don't foresee confronting Nan either. What would I accuse her of? Listening to a student?"

Magda cut in. "As I said, Irena could be her protégé. Keep your eyes open. If she is working with Nan, you'll no doubt see her scurrying in Nan's wake as she hustles around campus. My sense is that she overheard us and wanted to curry favor with her mentor."

T reached out and took Magda's hand. "My apology was too cursory. I want to tell you again, and in a heartfelt manner, how deeply sorry I am."

Magda smiled sweetly and allowed T to retain her hand. "Say three Hail Marys and an Act of Contrition, and sin no more."

T's eyebrows took flight. "I didn't know you were Catholic."

Magda shrugged. "I was raised Catholic. But I think that if I walked into a church now the ceiling tiles would rain down on me."

T gently pulled Magda toward him and hugged her affectionately. Maybe Clive was right. About things working out.

FIFTEEN

THERE FOLLOWED A PERIOD of quiet. T went about his work—teaching, reading, advising students, updating his notes, attending the occasional meeting. The following week, after the class had finished its section on genetics, Bradley Maun reappeared. He sat quietly in the back of the room, either staring forward or looking out the window. But he never said a word, never raised a question. There was a deadened look in his eyes as if he were either in a trance or bitterly resigned. T didn't try to approach him, but he did watch as he marched out of class at the end of the period. And "march" was the operative word: he walked in a sort of abbreviated stride as if his movements had been programmed.

T asked himself what he should do, if anything. Talk to Nan? He didn't see that as a productive move, seeing as she seemed to have become an adversary. The college had a so-called "SST"—Student Support Team. They were the folks to alert if a teacher had a concern about a student. The only problem was that Nan was at the helm of the team. But he had to do something, didn't he? Or had the situation—if that's what it was—burned down to an ember, become something to be aware of but not alarmed by? T opted for a middle ground. When he got back to his office he booted his laptop and created a new document file, which he labeled "M." He then typed out all the details of what had transpired to date. He would continue to make entries, copying and pasting relevant emails as well, so long as he sensed the affair was unresolved.

T felt better for taking this step, for creating a running record. The act of writing, he knew, was therapeutic. Who was it who said, "I write to find out what I'm thinking"? John Ashberry? Kurt Vonnegut? Well, someone said it, and T knew, from his own writing, that it was true. One written thought prompted another, and on and on.

The day was a long one. T worked for a couple of hours on his online cancer course and then spent some time in the lab, prepping for next week's exercise. Occasionally Faye Mundy came in and out. She was an adjunct in chemistry and taught a slew of classes to stay afloat. She was short, round, and pleasant; but also quiet, capable and diligent. She went about her preps with machinelike efficiency. Usually, when their paths crossed in the lab the two of them did little more than nod and exchange routine, course-related chit-chat. "You ever get that Benedict's Solution to work, T?"

"Yes, but I also learned that I'm not a chemist and the results were middling."

"Yes, it's funny how you can use the same chemicals, follow the same procedure, and the darn stuff works one time but not the next."

T smiled. There was a role for such banter. It was oddly comforting, perhaps because it was an indication of normalcy, which was something T craved at the moment. And then he decided to juice things up a notch. "Faye," he said as she was lining up some reagent bottles in Germanic order, "do you have a student named Bradley Maun in any of your classes?"

She paused and tilted her head to the side. "Yes," she said. "He's in my intro chem course."

"Any impressions?"

Faye had returned to her bottles but was more than capable of multitasking. "Quiet. Cooperative. Keeping up with the work. Why do you ask? Are you having any problems with him?"

T was careful about giving the impression that there was a student issue he couldn't deal with. "I'm not sure. But I see that you're not, so that's a good thing."

Faye turned and threw him a studied look as if seeing him for the first time. She removed her glasses and rubbed her eyes. Then she smiled and replaced the glasses. "I wish I could get to know my students a little more, but it's all I can do to keep up with the teaching as it is. I do wonder about these silent students. I wonder what's on their minds."

"Yeah," said T. "Still waters run deep. At least sometimes."

"Well, let me know if I can be of any help."

"Will do."

T's work stretched into the early evening. He rarely lingered on campus so long, and the shortening days made him feel alone and forlorn. When he left the building it was already six-fifteen. There was a bit of skyglow in the distance and the most potent stars had begun to wink. It always struck T how quickly it got dark once the sun had targeted the horizon. It was like a curtain falling. And then came the chill of night.

T gave himself credit for staying on a little later. When he got up in the morning he wouldn't have to rush to school early to do any prep work. This was the thought on his mind as he approached his car, residing in the diffuse glow of one of the parking lot lamps. But that modest light was all it took for him to see that someone was sitting on the passenger side. T halted and squinted at the figure. It was a male, staring straight ahead with empty eyes and the hood of his coat up. In the poor light, he looked ashen. T's heart quickened. He took a breath and slowly walked up to the window. The figure didn't turn. He continued to stare ahead, into the void.

T rapped on the glass with a knuckle. "Bradley, please roll the window down." The vehicle was a vintage Ford with no bells or whistles. When Olivia had asked about a newer vehicle, T advocated for keeping this one. "If we ever drive off a bridge into a river, we'll be able to hand-crank the windows down to escape."

"Bradley." Louder now. "What are you doing in my car?" One of the graces about life in Maine was that he didn't have to lock his vehicle. Now he would have to reassess this practice.

No response. Was he alive? Yes, T could see his breath. It must have been as cold, or colder, inside the car.

T took hold of the door handle, but it was locked. "Unlock it,

Bradley," he said, with authority. "Please."

T took out his key, but as soon as he unlocked the door Bradley came to life and—*bang!*—slammed the button down.

What to do? T took a deep breath and looked about the parking lot. He didn't want to call the police, but there didn't seem to be an alternative. And then, a few rows away, he spotted a familiar figure. "Praveen!" he called. The small, dark-skinned man, almost invisible in the subdued light, looked up. He waved. T walked toward him. "Praveen, I have a situation on my hands. I guess I need a witness."

"Of course. What is it?"

T led Praveen back to his car. When they got there, Bradley was gone. Praveen looked up at T. "Yes?"

T glanced about the parking lot. "A student was sitting in my car. I didn't know if he was in distress or what, but he wouldn't leave."

"What did he want?"

T ran a hand over the back of his neck. "I just don't know. But when I saw him it scared the hell out of me. I didn't know if he was alive or dead."

"Do you know who it was?"

"Yes. His name is Bradley Maun."

Praveen hummed.

"You know him?"

"He's in my Algebra I class. He's struggling, but he won't accept any help, despite my repeated offers." As Praveen said this, he held out his palms, as if demonstrating to T what he meant by offering to help.

T appreciated this intelligence. "I wish that was the only problem I was having with him."

Praveen's eyes were bright with interest. "I'm sorry for you."

T smiled. "Don't be sorry for me. I don't think it's anything I can't handle."

"I can feel your consternation. I wish I could do something."

T shrugged and pulled the collar of his parka closed. "Maybe you had the right idea when you said you were giving in to the provost. I hope it gave you some peace of mind."

Praveen wagged a finger. "I'm not giving in. I'm giving *way* for a bit, but I assure you, I will continue to do things my way."

"Maybe you're on to something. A sort of feinting maneuver."

"I'm not so designing," said Praveen. "But I do believe in peace of mind. However, there is much to admire in your more assertive stand."

The two men stood in the dark and cold, regarding each other. T glanced about the parking lot one last time and then looked back at his friend and colleague. "I appreciate you, Praveen."

The mathematician gave a slight bow. "It is mutual," he said. "And if you still need a witness..."

T smiled benignly. A witness to what? For all Praveen knew, it had been a hallucination.

"You're very kind."

SIXTEEN

T's SLEEP WAS FITFUL. He couldn't get that image out of his head of Bradley Maun in his car, looking so, so… cadaverous. Jesus, what was he hoping to accomplish? If all he wanted to do was spook T, he had succeeded royally. When T got up his only thought was to note this incident in his M blog. He would also have to communicate it to the powers that be, to protect himself if nothing else.

He soon realized he would have his chance. When he took an early look at his email, front and center was a message from the provost. *Can you come to my office at three today?* Well, at least it was a request this time. Maybe that was a sign of improving relations. T wrote back. *I'll be there.*

He left the house. The day was another chill one as October continued its inexorable march toward the winter ahead. The trees were increasingly bare, except for the oaks which hung onto their crinkled, brown masses of leaves, a testimony to their vigor. And then there were the pines and firs, which stood their ground, looking green and robust, awaiting their cloaks of snow.

When he got to campus he took care of a few minor chores in his office before heading to his Introductory Biology lecture. He had been conditioned to immediately glance toward Bradley Maun's desk. He was absent. This didn't portend well for a successful outcome, grade-wise.

T finished his lecture on unique genetic phenomena without incident. He spoke about color blindness, albinism, and diseases, such as hemophilia, that were linked to gender. The students resonated to the energetic lecture and gave up their applause when T concluded. As they filed out, a few lingered to ask some questions about the material. These were usually the students least in need of further elucidation. The ones who struggled with the material were those who repeatedly glanced at the clock while T was teaching and were the first out the door once the class ended.

The only other thing on T's schedule before his three o'clock with the provost was his online cancer course, which he would tend from his office. On the way, he bumped into Boats. Almost literally. The man had his head down and was tramping through the fallen leaves. "Whoa," said T. "Reverse engines."

Ted Toth stopped and looked up. His face was contorted with something resembling grief. "Boats? You okay? You look like hell."

The man sniffed and looked off into the distance. "Ah, shit," he said. "Life doesn't get easier as we go along, does it?"

T shrugged amiably. "I'm not sure it's supposed to. We're just supposed to get better at handling it." As he said this he thought of Olivia. It just never went away, but he had learned to function despite it all.

"How did you handle your loss?"

T focused on Boats. He considered that it might have been marginally easier to handle if more of his colleagues had attended Olivia's funeral. As it was, he had never felt so alone in his life. He didn't know where he had found the strength to lower Olivia into a place that would soon be frozen ground. And now, standing in the chill, under a leaden sky, framed by barren trees, he was being asked the most pointed of questions by someone he deemed unsympathetic in many regards. "Boats…"

"I've always admired you," he interrupted. "I've never been jealous that the students like you so much."

Where was all this going? T took another stab at the issue. "Boats, have you suffered a loss? I didn't know…"

Boats sank his hands into his coat pockets. "I'm a sixty-five-year-old man," he sniffed. "I'll get through it."

T began once more. "Boats. Ted. I'm not sure what you mean by 'it.'" And then, lowering his voice, "Are you talking about a death?"

Boats looked intently at T, his eyes filling with tears. "Perhaps it would be easier if it were a death. At least there would be some closure then. But this ambiguous loss..."

T felt off-balance. He had never exchanged more than pleasantries and a few sentences about policy issues with the elusive Boats. But now, here he was, interacting at a deeply emotional level with a man he hardly knew. He felt some shame at what he had to say next. "I'm sorry, Ted, but I have to teach. Can we get together when we're both free?"

Boats laughed in a subtle, off-hand manner. "It doesn't matter," he said. "I'll get through it."

T watched as his colleague trudged off, his shoulders slumped. He called out, "I'm willing to talk," but the man, without turning, simply waved a hand of acknowledgment over his head and continued to shuffle through the fallen leaves.

The encounter occupied T to his office. He wondered about the burdens that everyone carries, the things one is unable to shake, the knots one is unable to untie. He was in a state of mind where he was continually struggling to take care of himself. How on earth could he even begin to take care of someone else? And yet, that's what it was all about, no? Losing oneself in the other if for no other reason than to stay ahead of one's demons.

For the next hour, he immersed himself in his online course, correcting assignments and fielding questions from bewildered students. As inevitably happened from time to time, he caught a plagiarizer. Due to the general decline in student writing ability over the years, a well-wrought paragraph stood out like a sore thumb and T knew immediately that it wasn't the student's work. It was then a matter of copying and pasting the suspicious passage into the search engine, and in a twinkling, he had the source. When he delivered this intelligence to the offender, the student bristled and denied everything. Calmly, and with practiced clarity, T informed him of his good fortune in addressing this at the course level. "If you persist in your denials, I will pass this issue on to the dean, and he will not be so lenient. All I'm doing is giving you a zero for the assignment and warning you to copy no more." It was a sad and ugly business. With the advent of computer resources, the talent once known as "synthesis" had all but disappeared, and students genuinely believed that copying and pasting from the internet was a legitimate way to proceed.

The coursework done, additional papers corrected, a slew of emails answered, T reminded himself to send that email to Bradley Maun, inquiring as to his intentions in Introductory Biology. He copied the registrar and made the appropriate entry in his M file. Then he pulled out the chicken salad sandwich he had made and quietly ate at his desk. When Olivia was alive they would rendezvous for lunch in the faculty lounge, enjoying a peaceful meal, commiserating, and then, after a kiss, parting ways and returning to their work. It was a pleasant, reassuring rhythm, and it had evaporated.

Now T's thoughts were on three o'clock. He felt an unease about meeting with the provost again, especially after that first unhappy encounter. He wondered what this meeting would entail. He had every intention of mentioning Bradley Maun, especially the parking lot incident. In the interim, he buried himself in the lab, working apace until the appointed hour approached. T arrived in the provost's anteroom exactly on time. Peg greeted him brightly as if he were much-needed comic relief. "It's so good to see you, Professor!" she gushed, her worn expression improving when he walked into the room. T considered how difficult it must be to work for a man who was difficult to please.

"You too, Peg. Always a pleasure. Well, I don't want to be late..."

"Go in," she said, a curious note of caution in her voice. "I'll see you again shortly."

T gave a slight bow and ventured, "It's always easier to go in there after the delight of speaking with you."

Peg looked about, flustered, as if T had asked for her hand in marriage. He walked past her desk and went through the door. Then he halted. What was this? The provost was seated behind his desk, but there were three others in attendance as well. To the left sat Nan Hays. To the right, that student Magda had called Nan's protégé. What was her name? Irene? No, Irena. And then, perched off in a corner, like a decoration, was Bradley Maun, his eyes characteristically empty.

The provost gestured. "Come in, Professor," he said, warmly. "We're happy to see you."

T stood rigidly in place. "I feel at a disadvantage. I thought this was going to be a private meeting."

"It is private," said the provost, his head bobbing. "We're the only ones here."

T was having none of the man's semantics. "I mean, I thought this would be a one-on-one meeting."

Lawrence Graveline shook his head. "But that would entail speaking about people behind their backs. I thought it best to bring them here."

T focused on Irena, who kept glancing at Nan for affirmation. "With all due respect, I do not see what Irena has to do with whatever we are going to discuss."

Lawrence Graveline remained pleasant and unperturbed. "She has information..."

T put up a hand. "Again, with all due respect, Provost, let me be blunt. If she doesn't leave, I will leave."

Irena threw Nan a panicked look. But T was resolute and had no intention of accepting a situation where he was already outnumbered. As for Nan, she was seething. The thing he knew was that he had to remain composed and clarified, which would give him an immense advantage in any discussion in which others were driven by their anger. He wanted to be the reasonable party, but this did not mean yielding to every demand or request.

T watched as the provost and Nan leaned their heads together for a few moments. Then he returned to T. "Very well," he said, resigned. Turning to Irena: "There's no reason we should take up more of your time. We will let you know if you can be of further help."

Irena got to her feet and moved quickly for the door, taking pains to avert her eyes from T.

"Is this good now?" asked the provost, unctuously, as if he had just fluffed T's pillow.

"It's better," said T as he walked forward. There was a solitary chair positioned before the desk. T sat down and regarded his inquisitors. "Since I don't know what this is about, I'll wait for you to start the conversation."

Lawrence Graveline continued in his friendly tone, not showing any of the rancor he had displayed during their prior meeting. Perhaps he was putting his best foot forward for Nan's sake, intent on showing that he was not an unreasonable man. He glanced over at the corner. "You know this student, Bradley Maun?"

T nodded. "Yes. He's in my Introductory Biology course. But he's taken pains to introduce himself in other ways as of late."

The provost's eyebrows rose. "Oh? What do you mean?"

"There have been two incidents. You already know about the first one that took place on the mall."

"Yes," said the provost. "When you say he ran off when you approached him."

"Let's just say he walked away briskly. But the second incident happened just last night. I was working late. When I went to my car Bradley was sitting in the passenger seat."

"Oh?" Turning to Bradley Maun. "Is this so?"

"It's a lie."

T was taken aback, not only because of the denial, but it was the first time he had heard Bradley Maun's voice. It was thin and reedy, restrained as if his windpipe were too narrow. T looked intently at the provost. "I'm telling you he was sitting in my car. I tried to speak with him, but he wouldn't respond. When I tried to unlock the door he pounded on the button."

"Button?" peeped the provost. "What button?"

T sighed. "It's an old car. It has mechanical buttons for locking the doors."

"Oh." Lawrence Graveline shuffled some papers on his desk. "Well, you say he was in your car and he says he wasn't. This sounds like a case of he said-he said." And with this, he smiled in a self-satisfied manner.

"Now, wait a minute," objected T. "Why on earth would I make up such a story? I'm sitting here, senior faculty, full professor, with an impeccable record, and in the corner—and I hope Bradley will forgive me—you have someone failing my biology course who refuses to discuss his difficulties with me, and you're saying his word is as good as mine?"

Lawrence Graveline looked suddenly pained. "You say he was in your car. Do you have any witnesses?"

"Yes. Yes, I do. Praveen Khatri. He was in the parking lot too. I called him over expressly to act as a witness."

"And he saw this student in your car?"

T paused. "Bradley left by the time Praveen came over. But he was witness to my consternation."

"Professor…" said the provost in a pitying manner.

Nan had been listening intently to the conversation and finally spoke up. "I think we're getting off track here."

T regarded her with great interest. "Nan, I don't know why you're here, but I do think it's a good thing. I've always respected your work…"

"Except when it deals with brain physiology," she interrupted.

T leaned back in his chair. "Now who's getting off track?"

That was a mistake. Nan bristled. T watched as her hands balled into fists. For a psychologist, she had remarkably little self-control. "Now, you listen…"

Lawrence Graveline raised his hands. "Now, now," he said, again like a caring, considerate elder, "let's pause for a moment, take a breath, and press 'reset.'"

T knew it was to his advantage to not volunteer anything. It wasn't his responsibility to get the ball of conversation rolling again. So he sat, and pondered, and stole occasional glances at Bradley Maun. He looked on as the provost licked his lips and again shuffled his papers. Finally, "I did receive your syllabi. Thank you."

T nodded once. He resisted the impulse to check his watch.

"I think it's important not to take our eyes off the ball. This whole thing started when Mr. Maun registered a grievance that you, Professor, had said something about..."—and here the provost referred to one of his documents—"...yes, here it is. Something about our only reason for existence being to pass on our genes."

T didn't know whether to laugh or cry. He hoped his pained expression was not belying his incredulity. "It wasn't quite that simply put," he said. "Do I really need to spell it out all over again? I'd appreciate it if you'd just tell me what this student's issue is." And then he turned to Bradley Maun. "No," he said. "I'd like to hear it from Bradley himself. Bradley, why did what I said upset you?"

The three who were seated around the provost's desk looked on as Bradley sat up even straighter. He began to tighten the muscles in his neck as if he were struggling to swallow an oversized object. The others watched as he squinted and strained. Finally, and with great effort, he emitted two words. "I'm gay."

T continued to gaze at the distressed student. Then he turned back to Nan and the provost. "I don't understand. What does this young man's sexuality have to do with me?"

Nan seized the moment. "It has nothing to do with who you are, T," she said, disdainfully, as if frustrated that she needed to be instructive on the point. "It has to do with what you said."

T, against his better judgment, "I said that, as far as nature is concerned, living things exist to pass on their genes to their offspring. And I hastened to add that humans have other reasons for living as well." T all but bit his lip. He had just inferred that he didn't want to spell it out all over again, but here he was, spelling it out all over again.

Nan made sad eyes. "You just don't understand, do you?"

T recognized this game. He knitted his brow and conjured his own sympathetic expression. "No, Nan, I guess I don't. Please help me to understand." And then, seizing upon his momentum, he threw another glance at Bradley Maun. "Bradley," he said, "you're going to see that your professors also disagree from time to time, but we do so in a measured, respectful, civil manner." Returning to Nan and the provost. "Isn't that right, colleagues?"

He seemed to have paralyzed them. For some moments nobody said a word. Finally, Nan spoke up, addressing Bradley Maun. "Please tell Professor Tarnaszewski, in your own words, why you were so deeply wounded."

T caught fire. "I object," he said, "to someone else characterizing this student as deeply wounded. If Bradley is wounded, I would like to hear it from him."

Nan's mouth formed into a perfectly round O. She brought up her hands as if fending off an assault. T took up the slack. "Bradley, this is your opportunity to speak." Through all of this, the provost seemed to be struggling to maintain the composure he had committed himself to.

Again, Bradley strained at the neck, as if lacking sufficient oxygen. T now felt sorry for him. This was clearly a young man with personal challenges. But T was intent on not taking responsibility for them. He was willing to listen, not impale himself.

When the boy did find his voice, it turned remarkably clear and resonant. The reediness was gone. "I will never pass on my genes to any offspring. You condemned me."

That was it. T had never taken a student to task and he had no intention of starting now. He was aware of the tremendous advantage he had over these young people, and he had never sought to exploit it. But Bradley Maun seemed to have labored mightily to find personal insult in a fundamental, dispassionate matter of biology.

T hung his head, examined his hands, and began to speak. "What I said in class was not directed at any individual. It is good science and represents standard understanding of the central role of genetics in the lives of all living things. It's nothing that I haven't said before, during forty years of teaching this material." And then, looking up, "Does anyone really believe that any species can go on if it doesn't reproduce?"

Bradley whimpered. Tears were rolling down his cheeks and his shoulders were heaving. Nan jumped to her feet and flew to him. In a motherly fashion, she helped him up and put an arm around him. "I think Bradley should sit outside with Peg. We can continue this discussion without causing him any further pain."

T calculated that it was best not to respond to the veiled jibe. He watched as Nan, still with her arm around Bradley Maun, slowly shuffled out the door. A minute later she returned and resumed her seat on the provost's right. Slowly but surely the two sides were becoming more equitable.

"That was difficult," said Nan. Lawrence Graveline concurred. He raised his eyes to T. "As you can see, we need to handle this student with great care."

T measured his words. "My impression is that he's deeply troubled in a way that goes beyond anything I said in class."

Nan snapped, "Again, you're trying to play the clinician."

"Nan, your comment about being deeply wounded was uncalled for. You made it sound like I bludgeoned him with a blackjack."

"Well, you might just as well have. He's gay. Why weren't you sensitive to this?"

T threw up his hands. "I had no idea. Am I supposed to be asking these students about their sexual orientation? You make it sound like being gay is a disability. Or don't you believe that all people should be treated equally, given the same opportunities, and that their sexuality is none of my business?"

Nan would not be put on the defensive, but when she opened her mouth to reply, T looked pleadingly at Lawrence Graveline. "I still don't understand what the issue is. So Bradley is gay. There are probably other gay students in the class. They didn't seem to have a problem with my lecture."

Nan struck. "You basically told this student that he has no reason to live because he can't pass his genes on to any offspring." She looked triumphantly at T, as if she knew there could be no valid reply to such an insightful assertion. T was quick to disappoint her.

"Really?" he said. "That's the issue? Besides the fact that he can, indeed, reproduce if he so chooses, I am not going to alter a basic tenet of biology because one student has decided to feel uncomfortable about it. It would be like a history professor avoiding the subject of slavery if one of his students is black."

Nan blew her nose into a tissue, which she then waved at T. "Oh, please, it's not like that at all."

T turned to Lawrence Graveline again. “Provost, where do we go from here?”

Without hesitation, “Back to square one. First, you apologize to this student. Second, you immediately install the necessary trigger warnings in your syllabus.”

T clapped his hands together. “Well,” he said, “that makes things easier.” Leaning forward, he fixed both parties with his gaze. “The answers are ‘no’ and ‘no.’” He rose and turned to go. Lawrence Graveline, losing control now, barked after him. “This is insubordination. There will be a hearing.”

T turned back toward the desk. “I hope so,” he said. “I damn well hope so.” And then, addressing Nan, “I don’t know exactly what your role in all this is, or what your interest in this student is, but I will do my best to find out.” He left the office and paused momentarily to say goodbye to Peg, who seemed beset. It was clear she had once again heard everything. Then he turned to Bradley, who was sitting in a chair in yet another corner. Composed now, he had resumed his habit of staring into space. “Bradley,” said T, “I don’t expect you to respond to me, but students with difficulties usually go to the professor first. Failing that, there’s all sorts of help available to you. I’m still willing to have a conversation with you, but you shouldn’t expect me to change either the content or message of my course. Well, that’s all I have to say. If you speak, I’ll listen.”

Bradley Maun didn’t say a word. T continued on his way, with only one thought in mind. *Olivia, if you could see me now.*

SEVENTEEN

T FELT LIT, ENERGIZED. It was as if he were suddenly given a reason to live. Perhaps all he needed was a good fight. No, that's not right. That's not what he needed. But he couldn't have what he needed. This would have to do. He had never thought of himself as a fighter. Olivia had always done the fighting for both of them. She was a tried-and-true tomboy from New Jersey who had wandered to Maine—thank God—for peace of mind. Having had enough of the traffic, and industry, and crowding, and crime, and general in-your-faceness that characterized the Jersey streets, she had come north where she could walk more slowly, speak in a more measured fashion without somebody else inserting a paragraph, and get just about everything she needed at Wake's General Store, where she was known by name and could run a tab. Maine was, in short, one of those places one aspired to, and T was eternally grateful that Olivia had taken note of this exclamation point on the map of the United States. There weren't many of them. Maybe Oregon was another. But did anyone ever say, *Honey, someday we're going to sell everything and live the good life in Jersey?* Or Delaware? That's what they said about Maine. *Hell, let's chuck it all and move to Maine. We'll make do.*

This thought accompanied T back to his teaching lab, where he needed to re-pickle some fish specimens for the marine bio course he would teach in the spring. When he entered the prep room Faye Mundy was seated at a lab bench, pouring some agar plates from a hot flask for her microbiology section. "Hello, T," she sang without taking her eyes from her work. And then she sighed. "Autumn's holding up out there. It's too good a season to be sad in."

"Excuse me?" Was she talking to him? "I'm not sad." Actually, he was, in a way, but he didn't think it showed.

"Not you. Did you hear about Ted Toth?"

T drew closer to Faye, still with her eyes on her steaming plates. "I ran into Ted a short while ago. I could see that something was wrong, but he didn't say much. It felt like a death."

Faye put down the flask of hot agar, removed her protective glove, and swung about on her swivel chair. "I'm sorry. I thought you would have known. He and Nan Hays had a terrible breakup."

T was bowled over by this intelligence. "Ted and Nan? They were an item?"

Faye brought her hand to her mouth. "Oh, my. I'm sorry I said anything. Why did I think it was common knowledge? They were together for five years."

This was extraordinary. It seemed like such a monumental mismatch: Ted on his boat at every opportunity and Nan working non-stop, every day, long into the night, including weekends. When exactly did they have time to see each other?

"Well, I'm sorry to hear this. I wonder if I should say something to him. If I do, he'll want to know where I found out."

Faye was sympathetic. "Or he'll just think you're being a friend."

T looked away and ran a hand over his face. "That's just it. We're not friends. We're friendly, but we're not friends. It's hard to get my footing with this, although I'd like to help."

Faye arranged her plates on an enamel tray and moved to stow them. "Ask him out for a drink."

"I appreciate how much drinks oil relationships, but I'm at a disadvantage because I don't drink."

She stowed her things and hung up her white lab coat. "Then have a hot chocolate. His pain is palpable. Even if you're not friends, he could use somebody."

T nodded. "You're right. People are so damn busy. We've lost sight of what matters. Thanks, Faye. I'll say something to him."

"The sooner the better. When I saw him today he looked like he was going to cry."

Faye went on her way and T turned to his fishes. But he couldn't get it out of his mind. *Ted and Nan? Really? Boats? And Nan? How is it possible?*

The task took a good hour. When he was done, T looked at all those pickled bodies submerged in their jars of preservative, their lifeless eyes staring into the nothingness. Bradley Maun came to mind. Those eyes of his. Not quite lifeless, but certainly lightless. If T thought that putting a hand on the boy's shoulder and offering to be a mentor to him would help, he'd do it. But he didn't dare touch him. What if he cried out? Accused T of assault? Anything was possible these days. When T was twenty-six and just starting out, a young female student had come to his office, ostensibly about her grades. She had broken down in tears and threw her arms around him. His impulse was to return the gesture, but there was something desperate and mammalian in the embrace. He had conjured the emotional strength to firmly remove her hands. "What?" she demanded as she stepped back from him, sniffing and wiping her tears with her wrists. "What's wrong with you?" All T could say in response was, "I think you're going to be okay." Then he immediately reported the incident to the then-dean, who assured him that he had done the right thing, in the interest of protecting himself. T was grateful for the affirmation, but at some level, he felt abnormal. Any other healthy, virile, twenty-six-year-old would have at least reciprocated the hug. Today, if a student were to accuse him of an indiscretion, no matter how false the allegation, the college would cut him loose in a heartbeat. Did the students know how much power they had? It had become T's policy, when a student was in his office, to leave the door wide open. Female or male, it didn't matter. They were all now living in a nation of suspects.

When T got back to his office there was an email burning on his screen. It was from the provost:

> *I see from your schedule that you are free Monday at 1. Meet in my office. The dean will be there, as well as the president. Please acknowledge.*

The president? Well, if nothing else the provost was efficient. T responded that he would be there. Then he sent Magda an email asking if she was free for dinner Saturday evening. She must have been perched at her screen, because the reply was immediate. *Of course. How about Italian at Tesoro's? BTW, you hear about Ted and Nan? (Delete this email!)*

Everyone seemed to know about Boats and Nan. Maybe T's ignorance was the fruit of his minimalist approach to meetings, where most of the scuttlebutt was swapped. But beyond this, T was intrigued by Magda's closing gloss. *Delete this email!* Why? Because of the Ted tidbit? Or the idea that they were meeting for dinner? If the campus was abuzz with the news of Ted and Nan, was it also conjuring gossip about him and Magda?

What a world.

EIGHTEEN

SATURDAY AFTERNOONS WERE SACROSANCT. At precisely four o'clock T went to the cemetery and sat on the stone bench he had placed at Olivia's grave. He didn't well up with emotion during these visits. On the contrary, he found them comforting, almost uplifting. The Hope Grove Cemetery was nothing like the stupefying, card-catalog clusters of stones that constituted cemeteries in most urban areas; rather, it was one of those lovingly landscaped, garden variety affairs, with weeping willows, waterways, and wander paths, that had been established after the Civil War.

As T stared at Olivia's grave, two young teens on skateboards zizzed by. They were wearing their ball caps backwards and their butts stuck out of their drooping jeans. But this wasn't a criticism. This was how these places, these garden cemeteries, were meant to be—not only peaceful and comforting but democratic. The living were supposed to dwell here with the dead.

His mind meandered among recollected images of Olivia. A painful one showed up. Her last hour. He, seated by the side of her bed, holding her hand, his forefinger on her pulse. He could feel it ebbing, and he couldn't help but wonder which feeble throb would be the last. The tears were streaming down his face, but Olivia, so sallow and drawn, had mustered a last smile. "Oh, T," she said, in a bare whisper, "you've just got to let me go."

T continued to stare at the stone. His name and birth year were already engraved under Olivia's. Before her passing, he had always thought that such things were rather ghoulish. But now he understood. He was no longer a believer, but this much he did have faith in: that one day the stonemason would return to this very spot, kneel by this very stone, and insert the year of his death.

Twilight came and with it the evening winds. T zipped his parka up to his neck, got to his feet, and walked back to his car. There were only a few other people in the cemetery, walking the paths, disappearing around the gentle hills, or ascending the granite steps of one of those hills. T made a mental note to make a more thorough exploration himself one day. But for now, it was time to go home and get ready to meet Magda at Tesoro's.

NINETEEN

As T GOT READY to leave the house, he couldn't help wondering if his meeting Magda for dinner—in a restaurant, no less —constituted a date. He dispelled the thought, especially as he had just returned from the cemetery. Was he one of those survivors who were buried along with the deceased spouse, with the result that he was incapable of loving another person in anything but a platonic way? Olivia knew first-hand of his capacity for love—he had been so abjectly devoted to her. But she was not the type to demand a deathbed promise from him never to romance another woman. T shed the word "romance" with a shake of his head. Tootsie scurried into the room while he was changing his clothes. She jumped up onto the bed and eyed him curiously as he combed his still-thick hair. T turned and regarded the animal, watching as she licked a paw, yawned, and then snuggled down into the bedspread, her eyes—those uniquely cattish eyes—closed in sweet bliss. One of T's students had an accommodation to bring a pug named "Chubbs" to class as his emotional support animal. Was this what Tootsie was? Emotional support? She was already ten years old. What would happen when she died? Would he have to get another cat? Would he be one of those people who bury their cats in a pet cemetery?

When T got to Tesoro's Magda was already there, sitting in a booth, reading a book. Only a few tables in the large space were occupied by diners. The hostess was a full-bodied, middle-aged woman named Mirabella. She was notoriously curt. The scuttlebutt was that she wanted to return to Brooklyn, but her husband, Bruno, who was the co-owner and sole cook, wouldn't leave Maine. When Mirabella spotted T she approached him with a cold eye, the frills on her muumuu undulating like the fins of a predatory fish. "Do you have a reservation?" she demanded.

T looked about. "Reservation? The place is almost empty."

Mirabella didn't take prisoners. "Still," she said, "you must have a reservation."

"T!" Magda was waving him over from her redoubt in the booth.

"There's my reservation." Mirabella narrowed her eyes as T walked around her. He took his coat off and sat opposite Magda. "Thanks for rescuing me. She's got to be the rudest hostess I've ever met."

Magda smiled. "It's the price we pay for Bruno's pasta puttanesca."

"Then we're over-taxed." Turning his attention to Magda, he smiled. "Well, here we are."

"Let's take a look at the menu first so we can stake our claim to food. We don't want to give Mirabella a reason to throw us out."

"You said puttanesca. That sounds good to me." The server came and took their orders.

Magda was still smiling brightly. "How goes the battle?"

T lifted a shoulder. "The enemy mounted a frontal assault but I think our line is holding. For now."

He could see that Magda was working to sustain her smile. He wished she didn't regard him as someone who needed cheerful encouragement. "I had another meeting with the provost. Only this time, when I walked in, Nan was there, along with the student, Bradley Maun, and that young woman who had eavesdropped on our conversation and dutifully reported to her *Gauleiter*." T knew he was being unkind with that last comment, but he needed someone he could speak to in an unfiltered manner. Besides, he owed it to Magda to show that he trusted her.

"Why was Nan there?"

"First things first. I asked that Irena be excused. I prevailed, but nobody was happy about it."

"Go on."

"To make a long story short, I finally found out why Bradley Maun was so aggrieved. By the way, did I tell you that I found him sitting in my car the other night?"

"Whoa, whoa," said Magda, leaning forward. "In your car? What was he doing in your car?"

"That's the sixty-four-thousand-dollar question."

"What did you do?"

"I tried to talk to him but he sat there like a zombie. When I tried to open the door he locked it again."

"Oh, T…"

"Let me get back to the meeting." Before he said another word the server, an older woman with a severe aspect, brought their drinks and salads. T had to lean back as she fussed with the utensils and place settings in a manner suggesting she resented the task. "Well," said T after she had gone, "it turns out that Bradley is gay."

"So?"

"Yes," nodded T. "That was my response. So? But Bradley actually spoke, and if he weren't causing me such grief it would have broken my heart the way he struggled to get his words out."

Magda was slowly shaking her head. "What does his being gay have to do with anything?"

"Again," said T as he lifted his fork, "that was my response. Bradley said that I had condemned him when I said, in class, that living things exist to pass on their genes to their offspring. He said I had condemned him because he would never pass on his genes."

Magda blinked several times as if to dispel something she was uncertain of. "But you weren't talking about him."

T speared an onion and held it aloft. "Of course not. But the provost still wants me to apologize to him. And then there are those damned trigger warnings." He ate the onion and glanced over at Mirabella, who was working the cash register. For all her failings, the salads at Tesoro's were top-notch.

"What was the resolution?"

"Bradley broke down and Nan took him out of the room. Then I told the provost that I would neither apologize nor give trigger warnings. He threatened me with a hearing for insubordination." With this, T dug into his salad with gusto.

Magda watched him eat for a few moments. "Well, it hasn't affected your appetite. That's a good thing."

T paused and glanced at her. "They say that people eat to alleviate depression."

"Are you depressed?"

T sat up and put his fork down. "You know, I think I can honestly say that I'm not. If anything, I feel energized. Not necessarily in a good way, because I'm on edge, but circumstances have forced me into the breach."

"The breach?"

"Yes. On Monday I meet with the provost, the dean and—if you can believe this—the president."

"The president!"

"Magda, it's not an honor. The guy's an enigma. The only time we see or hear from him is when he's scolding us. The problem is, some really resonate to the strong hand, to toughness."

Magda took her fork and started to poke at her salad. "Oh, I don't know," she said. At that moment Mirabella came over. She focused on T. "Try not to be too long. We have a big group coming in."

T threw her an incredulous look. "We haven't even gotten our meals yet."

Mirabella was unmoved. "Bruno is very busy. Be patient." Then she drifted away.

T shook his head. "This place should be called 'Mussolini's.'"

Magda laughed. "As you said, some people like the strong hand. Ah, here's the puttanesca."

The server put the plates down. "Watch it, lady, it's hot."

Magda took the first bite and sighed. "Ambrosia." And then, "Do you have a game plan?"

T shrugged. "I'll stand my ground. I'll be outnumbered, but I know my mind in this messy business. I don't think I could live with myself if I gave in now." With that, he tasted a forkful of the puttanesca. "This pasta is delicious!" He swallowed and mused, "I wonder if that's what condemned men say when they taste their last meals?"

Magda had no response to that. "You still haven't told me why Nan was there."

T wiped his mouth with a napkin. "I've been thinking about this. Early on, the provost told me that Bradley Maun—well, actually, he said 'a student'—had registered a complaint. But I don't think Bradley went to the provost. I don't even think he knows what a provost is."

"You think that Nan…?"

"I know she was royally pissed off about two things: my not applauding her brain talk, and then criticizing her outright in my conversation with you in the faculty lounge."

Magda had ceased eating. "I can't believe she would be so vengeful. I mean, we're a community of scholars, and we care about each other."

T regarded her with compassionate eyes. *Dear, dear Magda. You babe in the woods.* "Magda, I mean no offense, and take this as a sign that I trust you implicitly, but don't you think the academy can be a pit of vipers? Yes, it's been good to me, and I enjoy my students, most of my colleagues, and the opportunities for advancement and personal development. But all the whispering, conspiracy, and machinations. It's like people feel constantly compelled to compare genitals."

Magda grimaced and then emitted a low, plaintive peep as if her skin had been pricked.

Maybe he couldn't be so candid with her after all. He didn't think the wound was mortal, but he regretted having wounded her at all. And yet, he wanted to be able to say what was on his mind. At least with one person. He smiled. "Can you imagine how much I'd be running off at the mouth if I drank?"

Magda conjured her own smile and rekindled her stock in trade—the search for the silver lining. "Everything will be okay," she said. "Things always work out for the best."

T had no stomach for platitudes, and if this weren't Magda he was sitting with, he would have challenged them now. "Well, yes, ultimately," he said as he returned to his puttanesca. The server reappeared at their table. "You folks having dessert?"

TWENTY

T WAS IN THE lab, sitting with a student who was struggling in biology. His issues were elementary and easily addressed, but T was distracted. Not by the looming meeting with the college's triumvirate, but by the dinner he had had with Magda. He liked her, he appreciated her, but he felt that he wasn't quite bringing her on board with his concerns. It was the perpetual sunniness that broadsided him. Just once he needed to be affirmed, to be told, *Yes, you're right. You're absolutely right. They're brutes.*

"Professor?"

"Hmm? Yes, do you understand this question now?"

The student was a young man with a brilliant smile framed by a terrible complexion. This was his first semester in college and T could see how at sea he was.

"No, I don't get it."

T looked the boy over. Whenever he had a student he was having trouble getting through to, he pictured himself at eighteen. Although he had done well in high school, college—Princeton, of all places!—had hit him like a ton of bricks. It took him the entire first semester to get his act together, rise to the challenge of very complicated material, and learn to take notes in a lecture hall with two hundred other students and no opportunity to ask questions. No professor had offered to sit down with him after class and entertain his doubts. Certainly not the imposing, austere Professor Rudy, his botany prof. On one particularly difficult exam, T had made a stupid error, completing only two essays when three were required. How could he have overlooked that directive? In a panic, he had made a mad dash to Rudy's office, where he pleaded for an opportunity to address the third question. "Please, Dr. Rudy. I'm just asking for a chance. I know the material!"

Professor Rudy, a giant of a man at six-foot-ten, gazed passively over the lanky, trembling T's head and quietly but sternly issued his response: "You should read the instructions."

That was it. No mercy. T managed to just pass the test based on his other two essays, but his professor's intransigence turned him into an obsessive-compulsive when it came to his schoolwork. His subsequent semesters were stellar, and, three years later, he graduated magna cum laude, to the immense satisfaction of his weeping parents.

And now here he was, sitting next to a student, going over his work line-by-line, giving him the benefit of every doubt, functioning in equal parts as teacher, mentor, and social worker. He realized that this student was in no way prepared for college. His reading skills were poor, his writing garbled, and his basic comprehension marginal. Willis Rudy wouldn't have stood for it.

"Do you see that you mislabeled this cell structure, Jason?" T all but took the boy's index finger in hand to lay on the diagram. "Do you see this?"

Jason, his voice full of doubt, peeped, "Yes." And then, "I think."

T reached into his folder and laid a sheet before the lad. "These are the solutions. I want you to go home, compare them to your work, and circle anything that's unclear. Then we'll look at it again if you need further clarification. How does that sound?"

The boy, his smile glowing in that galaxy of skin lesions, nodded. "Okay," he said. "Thank you for spending so much time with me."

Again, T looked him over and saw himself, minus the obvious deficiencies. "You're worth it, Jason." He watched as the boy gathered his things and left the room.

And now he faced his own reckoning. Shortly, he would again go to the provost's office to gather what he assumed would be some sort of decision on the part of the college. They couldn't fire him; tenure was a potent shield and he was sure they wouldn't squander scarce resources trying to penetrate it. But there were other ways to discipline a faculty member. These were the thoughts that preoccupied T as he left the room. "Oops! Excuse me!"

He had stepped right into the path of Faye Mundy, who had a flask in each hand. She stood there, squat and round, in her lab coat, holding the vessels aloft. "No harm done," she said. "It's not nitroglycerine." Then she gathered T in. "You look harried. Off to the races?"

T, distractedly, "Off to be run over."

"Ouch. Anything I can do?"

Faye was still holding the flasks aloft, like the scales of justice. T noted a genuine sense of concern in her voice. "No, no. Maybe at some point I can fill you in. Sorry for being so scattered. I'm trying to pull my thoughts together."

He watched as Faye bent down and put the flasks on the floor. She stood up, opened her arms, and gave him a long, tight hug. T was all but paralyzed by the gesture, but he didn't resist, his chin resting on top of her head. "Faye..."

She released him and retrieved her flasks. "I thought you needed that."

T looked after her as she continued on to her class.

He checked his watch and headed for the provost's office. After exchanging the requisite pleasantries with Peg, he entered. The scene was intimidating: sitting dead center behind his desk was Lawrence Graveline. To his left sat the dean, Roger Olib, who seemed to be struggling to get comfortable in his chair. And to his right was the president, Ned Trumbull, in his signature red bowtie. He was the only one not looking up. Instead, he was paging through some documents on his lap and making marks with a pencil. It occurred to T that he should have demanded to have someone—perhaps a union rep—with him as a witness. Just in case.

Unbidden, T walked up to the desk and took a seat. The provost was not jocular this time. He turned to his right and left. "Professor Tarnaszewski, you know President Trumbull and Dean Olib?"

T was put off by the faux formality. He decided to be mischievous. "No, I'm afraid not." This threw Lawrence Graveline off. He shot quick, birdlike glances at the men flanking him. The dean was staring at T, licking his lips, but the president was still going over his papers, unperturbed, the picture of self-absorption.

Dean Olib barked at the provost. "Well, get on with it."

T stared at the dean and recollected, *I do not have a first-rate mind, but I do have a capacity for action.*

Lawrence Graveline, bookended by the president and the dean, looked smaller now, his head with its ring of red hair buried even deeper into his hunched shoulders, making him look like a frightened turtle. He played his fingertips on the desktop for a moment and then spoke up. "Professor Tarnaszewski, you knew this was coming. You were warned…"

The dean slammed his hand on the desk. "Damn it, Lawrence, stop beating around the bush. No preambles." He launched a finger at T. "You! You are being cited for insubordination and we intend to terminate you."

T pulled back as if he had absorbed some terrible blow to the head but was still, somehow, standing. He hadn't expected this. Maybe the dean was a man of action after all, no matter how ill-considered. T was boiling, absolutely boiling. Was it possible not to let it show? To maintain a semblance of dispassion? He felt a desperate tension that made him clench his jaw. Surely the others must have sensed blood in the water and would now circle in for the kill. T looked over at the president, who, remarkably, was still scribbling on his papers, legs crossed, head down. He was tapping his foot, rhythmically, as if a song were playing in his head. T struggled to remind himself of the immense advantage one had in any argument if one remained calm, thoughtful, and soft-spoken. But God almighty! *This!* He felt his head spinning off his shoulders. The impulse to scream out was overwhelming. He had never felt so alone. *My God… Olivia…* He took great care to not allow anyone to mistake his throat-clearing for a whimper. "This takes me by surprise. May I…may I ask a question?"

The president stopped tapping, looked up, and stared at T over the glasses perched on the tip of his nose. Then he glanced at the provost and nodded. "Ask your question," said Lawrence Graveline.

T spoke in such low tones that the provost and dean were compelled to lean forward. The president had returned to his papers and resumed tapping his foot, but he must have been listening.

"Is there a precedent for this?"

Roger Olib squinted. "For what? Precedent for what?" Then he slapped the desk again. T noted the disapproving glance this brought from the president.

T was careful not to shrug or to take his eyes from his interrogators. Every word, every gesture, had to be carefully calculated. He felt a weight on his chest and a tightness in his neck. Was it still possible to speak? It had to be. He spoke up with the cadence of a poet. "For firing a tenured, senior, award-winning, full professor with stellar teaching evaluations. For insubordination."

Lawrence Graveline looked at the dean, who was seething. He returned the provost's glance, the two seeming to confer at some telepathic level. The provost outranked the dean, and yet he was deferential toward him, his eyes pleading for direction as if he were simply outgunned by Roger Olib's rancor. Their silent communication went on for several long moments, during which T sat quietly and expectantly, making fists in his lap to dispel some of his stress. The only move the president made was to uncross his legs and then re-cross them in an opposing manner. All of this would be easier if only someone like Magda, or even Clive, were there with him. To share in his astonishment. To put the powers that be on notice that there were limits. And witnesses.

The moments wore on until the self-appointed man of action growled, "President Trumbull would have the answer to that."

All eyes turned to the president. Trumbull slowly raised his head and eyed T—but not directly, more to the side of his head—with that look of immense sadness so characteristic of the man. He also conveyed the sense that it was beneath him to communicate directly with that lower species known as faculty. Still, T was startled by both the content and the tone of his words. In a voice as dry as parchment, "We don't need any God-damned precedent. Your case will be the precedent." Then he lowered his head and returned to his papers.

Was it all so incidental, then? This process of firing? Was it all so easy and routine? T was convinced that it couldn't be. He didn't want to get lost in his ruminations, so he asked one last question: "Why are you doing this?"

The president didn't make a move. He was done speaking. Roger Olib nudged the provost to life. He bobbed his head. "Because you refused to cooperate. Because you're not a team player. Because you were warned. We asked for trigger warnings and you refused. That's deliberate disobedience against which your tenure is no shield. Need I go on?"

T felt a sudden surge of relief as if some of the weight had been lifted from his chest. That was all they had? Firing a tenured professor because he wasn't a team player? He spoke up. "I presume I have until the end of the semester?"

The provost and the dean registered the same expression— surprise at T's lack of resistance. Lawrence Graveline bobbed his head again. "Of course. We don't want to disrupt those classes of yours that are already in progress. For the students' sake."

Both men continued to look baffled as T got up. They seemed to be expecting him to say something, to fly off the handle. Was there a better reason not to say anything? His time would come. He turned and walked out the door, closing it behind him, only to find Peg quietly weeping at her desk. He put his arm around her shoulder. "Are you crying for me?" She nodded and sniffed in a ladylike fashion into her handkerchief. "Don't worry," added T. "It may not be as simple as all this."

When he got back to his office he sat at his desk for a few long minutes. His eyes wandered to his books, to the affirmation poster directing students to consider all the possibilities of a career as a biologist (*HORIZONS UNLIMITED!*), the preserved specimens in their neatly arranged jars, the fossil bivalves he had excavated from the Ohio River valley, and a poignant note from a student, which T kept at eye level on the wall over his desk: *Anyone can be a teacher, but it takes a special person to be a mentor and a friend.* And he knew he couldn't easily turn his back on all this. After another moment's thought, he picked up the phone, searched his contacts, and touched the screen. On the third ring came the jaunty greeting—"*Yello!*"

"Clive?"

"Russki! I don't think I've ever received a call from you. This is momentous. What's up?"

"I'm ready for that drink."

TWENTY-ONE

T DECIDED TO GO home early, something he rarely did. He was feeling remarkably well. Clarified. It must have been the dissipation of all the ambiguity. The die was now cast, the battle lines drawn, and he knew exactly what was at stake. He had arranged to meet Clive in the lounge of the Thai Lotus restaurant. A lounge! He knew what a lounge was, but, oddly, had never visited one. Not even with Olivia.

When T got to his house there was an official-looking vehicle parked out front. A young man, presumably the driver, was talking to one of the neighbors, Carol Pats. She was a notorious busybody, a self-appointed neighborhood sentinel, but she meant well, taking in stray cats as her mission in life. Whenever T needed to know something of local import, she was the go-to person. No team of wild horses was needed to drag the details out of her. And now, here she was, in her kerchief and pink fuzzy slippers, holding the collar of her faded duster closed with one hand while she gesticulated with the other, the young man listening intently and nodding.

T parked. When Carol Pats saw him she flew in his direction. "Oh, T!" she lamented. "It's terrible."

T knew that, for Carol, a pothole was a catastrophic failure of the powers that be, so he listened quietly. "It's okay, Carol," he said. "Just tell me what happened." She must have rushed out of her house in a panic because she wasn't wearing a coat on such a chilly day. He glanced over at the parked vehicle and saw the lettering on the driver's door. Animal Control. Turning back to Carol. "Is it a roadkill?"

She shook her head. "No. On your porch. A dead cat."

T's heart leaped into his throat. "Where? Carol, where is the cat?"

She resonated with his empathy. Now both of them were on the same page. "There," she said, throwing a finger toward Animal Control.

T went over to the man and identified himself. His heart was thumping and his palms were filling with sweat. "Please show me," he said.

The young man took T around to the back of the vehicle. He opened the door and there, lying in state, was a coal-black animal. There were no apparent signs of violence. "It wasn't attacked," he said. "Or run over. Must've been something it ate."

T looked up at his house and there, in the second-floor window, was Tootsie, staring down at him. He returned to Carol, whose tears were about to overflow their rims. He put a hand on her shoulder. "It was Benno," she sniffed, patting herself down in search of a tissue. T reached into his back pocket and gave her his handkerchief, which she seized gratefully. Then she raised her eyes to T. "I don't mean no disrespect," she said, "but I told you not to put cat food out on your porch."

T would sometimes allow Tootsie to take the air on the front porch. But she knew the limits of her range and never ventured down onto the sidewalk. "I don't understand," he said. "Even if Benno ate the cat food, it was the same stuff I feed to Tootsie."

Carol Pats waved him off with the handkerchief. "You don't understand," she protested. "I'm sure it was that boy."

"What boy?"

"That boy," she repeated. "I could see from my window. He went right up on your stoop. I saw him bend down, but I thought he dropped something. Then he hurried away. Oh, I should have been harder on Benno, but he liked to roam."

The pieces were falling together. "Carol, what did the boy look like?"

Sniffing. "It was hard to tell from across the street. He was dressed in black, with a hooded coat. When he turned, his hair was blowing across his face. Then he hurried away like he had someplace to go."

T took a moment. He looked around. Then his eyes settled on Carol Pats again. "I'm sorry," he said. "And I'll be sure to keep cat food off the porch."

She sighed deeply. "That's all I ask. But it ain't gonna bring Benno back." T watched as she crossed the street and returned to her home.

He examined the food dish on the porch. A portion had been eaten. He knew exactly what he needed to do, and in what order. He removed the cat food from the porch and divided it up into two small plastic containers. Then he called the police and gave them Bradley Maun's name. He was sure Carol Pats would act as a witness. Proceeding apace, he called Animal Control and told them to keep the cat refrigerated, as the police were now involved. Then he sat down at his computer, opened the M file, and made his entry. Last, he called his colleague over in chemistry, Hal Koch, and asked if he could assay one of the samples. "But you need to be careful, Hal. It's already killed a cat." Hal sounded excited at the prospect of some forensic intrigue. When T hung up, Tootsie stretched out against his leg. "How could I forget about you?" he said as he picked her up and hugged her to his chest. "No more going outside for a while."

The police showed up and T communicated everything he knew. Then he handed the officer one of the cat food samples. "Please be careful." He was to meet Clive Gridley at five at the Thai Lotus, but he still had a little time, so he sat down at the computer and drafted an email, which he directed to the president, the dean, the provost, and Nan Hays.

I have reason to believe that Bradley Maun tried to poison my cat. I have called the police. I am writing this email in the interest of full disclosure and to keep you in the loop.

T took a breath. He was now involved in serious business, and the threat of his termination was the least of it. If Bradley Maun had intended to kill Tootsie, then that meant he had been surveilling the house to ascertain the patterns of its inhabitants. He had probably seen Tootsie out on the porch at some point. T considered that he had every right to feel enraged, and frightened. But he was neither. The scientist in him counseled moderation, precision, and dispassion. Slowly but surely he was accumulating data. It wouldn't be long before he could offer up a theory based on that data. For now, he needed to rendezvous with Clive.

When he arrived at the Thai Lotus his colleague was sitting alone at a table in the corner of the pleasantly lit lounge. There were a couple of patrons at the bar, laughing. But only one other table was occupied, at the far end of the room. T reflexively glanced about for familiar faces. "*Hey!* Over here!"

Clive was so unselfconscious. On his feet, his tie was loose and one of his shirttails was hanging out. "Pull up a chair!"

T shook Clive's outstretched hand and was struck by how soft and meaty it was. Something in him wanted to hang onto it. But Clive withdrew the mitt and plopped down again. "We can eat too, you know," he said as if just figuring out that the lounge was part of the restaurant. "We don't have to just get a drink." He signaled to a young Thai woman. "Honey, could I get one of those real authentic Thai beers? And my friend here…?"

T was embarrassed by Clive's addressing the woman as "Honey" and hoped that his reddening sent her a message that he disapproved. "Just…just a club soda with a twist of lemon for me, thanks." He took pains to acknowledge the woman by looking at her as he spoke.

"Hey," said Clive, smiling, "I thought we were meeting for drinks."

"Clive, I need some advice."

The colleague's expression dropped. "This is one for the books," he said. "You asking me for advice."

"I know. Politics makes strange bedfellows."

"Ah, so this is about politics then."

Their drinks came. T caught Clive eyeing the menu lying next to him on the table. He was licking his lips. "Clive, if you want to eat…"

"Honey," said Clive, signaling to the waitress again. "A Pad Thai with chicken for me. And for my friend…?" T waved a hand. "Well if you don't mind watching me eat…"

"I don't mind."

"Okay then." He nodded the waitress away. Turning to T, "Lay it on me."

T, machine-gun style, recited his story from start to finish. He held nothing back. The biology class, the comment he had made about genes, Bradley Maun's reaction, the warning from the provost, Nan Hays's odd involvement, the snitching Irena, his termination. He ended with a description of the death of Benno and the subsequent email he had sent.

Through it all, Clive, to his credit, listened attentively. He never interrupted, never looked over T's shoulder to see who had entered the room. Instead, he took notes on a napkin, occasionally humming or nodding. Just as T finished, the waitress came with Clive's meal. T watched as he dug in like a man breaking a fast. He finally ventured, "Well, what do you think?"

Clive belched with something resembling pride that he could muster such a quantity of gas. Then he swiped out his mouth with an index finger. "You shouldn't have sent that email to the big four," he said. "At least not yet."

T thought for a moment. It's true, he had violated his principle that emails written in angry haste needed time to cool before they were sent off. "I just wanted to keep them in the loop."

Clive waved a finger at T while chasing a slice of water chestnut with his fork. "No you didn't," he said. "You wanted to check their king. But all you did was assert something you can't yet prove."

T had underestimated Clive. He had never heard him speak with such authority and self-assurance. His slovenly appearance and freewheeling ways belied what T was coming to see as talent. "Well, the deed is done."

"Yes it is," said Clive as he glugged a good third of his beer and wiped his mouth on his sleeve. "And who knows? Maybe it will give them something to think about. But you can't treat this like a game." Then he smiled devilishly. "That's my job."

"Your job?"

Clive, having cleared his plate, raised his hands. "You do want me to represent you, don't you?"

"Represent?"

Clive was in high gear. "There are monumental issues here. Academic freedom, wrongful termination, animal cruelty. We have our work cut out for us." He rubbed his hands together in anticipation of either the fight ahead or dessert.

T was moved by the prospect of a real, and capable, ally. "Clive, I…I don't know what to say."

"T, we're all in this together. There, I said it for you."

It was not lost on T that Clive had ceased calling him "Russki."

TWENTY-TWO

By the next morning, there still hadn't been a response from any of the recipients of that last email. Perhaps T had paralyzed them or at least given them pause to consider that the situation was not as simple as they perhaps thought.

T tended to Tootsie before leaving the house. He checked and re-checked the locks with the diligence of a paranoiac. He called Carol Pats, re-emphasized his sorrow at Benno's death, and asked if she would keep an eye out for any suspicious persons near his home.

When T got to his Introductory Biology class he froze on the threshold. There, in his appointed place, was Bradley Maun, sitting in his black bench warmer. This time he didn't have that deadened look but regarded T with interest and a Mona Lisa smile. T's heart began to race. Who knew what this kid was capable of? Who knew what he was harboring under his coat? School shootings were happening all the time. As were suicides. What was T's choice? That Bradley Maun kill him or kill himself? He didn't know what to do. If he called security, what would he tell them? That he didn't like this student? That he was uncomfortable having him in class? Then he would have to justify it. *He tried to kill my cat.*

He tried? Is this something you know?

Well…

A further question: Had the police approached Bradley and interrogated him? My God, there was an accusation of poisoning an animal to death. Why hadn't anyone contacted him and given him the result of the inquiry? T walked over to his desk. As he laid out his materials he stole glances around the classroom, laying his eyes on anything that might serve as a defensive weapon if need be. This is what it had come to then. A student had put him in a state of anxiety and abject fear. The task now was not to let it show.

The lecture topic was "Epigenetics"—the idea that the environment can shape the expression of one's DNA. As T pivoted between the board and his students, he knew his game was off. He dropped the marker twice and then lost his train of thought. "Oof," he smiled as he leaned back against the board. "This stuff is complicated, isn't it? Even I'm having difficulty getting it to hang together."

His students chortled good-naturedly. "Let's try this again." He returned to the board but mostly relied on muscle memory to allow his hand to sketch out the basic ideas. He was wrestling with his mind, trying to subdue the wayward thoughts of Bradley Maun that kept intruding. And then, *My God, I'm turning my back to him!*

T spun about so suddenly that he tripped over his own feet. The students gave a start and stared at him. T laughed through his nose. "Hey, I just wanted to see if you were still awake." And then he noticed that Bradley Maun was gone.

After the lecture, T sat down and put his head in his hands. *That was the worst lecture of my life.* He had stumbled, been disjointed, and generally unsure of what he wanted to say next. Was it all becoming too much? It was in moments like these that he missed Olivia more than ever. What would she say if she were here? She wouldn't pull a Magda and attempt to cheer him up. No, she'd say, *Let's get out of here for a while. We need a change of scenery.*

But we can't just leave campus in the middle of the teaching day.

Who says we can't? It's a saintly sin of delight.

T smiled into his hands. For a moment he thought he might shed a bitter tear of remembrance. A robust clap on the back jolted him back into the moment. "Don't do that!" he barked. "Geez, Clive..."

The jocular colleague presented his palms like a mendicant. "You looked like you needed some cheering up."

T firmed his jaw. "I do not need cheering up. And I do not want to be happy all the time."

Clive looked bewildered. "Calm down, my friend. I'm just here to tell you that we're going to meet with Boats."

T examined his colleague's face. "Boats?"

Clive rubbed his meaty hands together. "Oh, you're gonna love this, brother."

Brother. T wondered if he didn't prefer *Russki*. "I don't understand. What does Boats have to do with me?"

Clive laid a hand on T's shoulder in an affirming manner. "Maybe everything. Just tell me you're free tonight to meet at the Lotus. Boats likes having his gears oiled. I hope to have his engine purring like a kitten. We're meeting at six."

T nodded. "Sure. Okay. Do I need to prepare in any way?"

Clive was already headed for the door. He stopped on the threshold, turned, and shielded his mouth with a hand. In a harsh whisper, "Just fasten your seat belt."

All this intrigue. T gathered his things and retreated to his office. He called the police department and identified himself. "Did you find out anything?"

His call was passed among three officers. The third was very businesslike and his speech was choppy as if his words had been knit together from different sources, like a ransom note. T could hear papers shuffling at the other end. "Mr. Tarnaszewski," the officer said with some effort, laying heavy emphasis on each syllable. "We spoke with Mr. Maun."

Mister Maun. It gave the student a status T didn't think he deserved. "And?"

"Well, he denied everything."

"I had a witness. Mrs. Pats from across the street."

The officer continued in his businesslike manner. The man could have been one of those virtual assistants whose voice is programmed by a computer. "We spoke with Mrs. Pats. She couldn't give us a description of the suspect's face."

T hummed disconsolately. "Can't you search his house for poison?"

"We need probable cause for a search warrant. We would have a hard time convincing the judge."

The officer didn't seem hurried. T felt like he was willing to stay on the phone all day with him if necessary. Maybe he was interacting with a virtual assistant after all and the technology had simply become remarkable. "What about the cat food?"

"It's still in the lab."

"Won't that be proof?"

"Won't what be proof, sir?"

"If there's poison in it."

"It will be proof of poison, but not proof that Mr. Maun put it there."

T couldn't help smiling in silly disbelief at the ping pong nature of the conversation. He started to line up question upon question in his head, wondering how long he could keep the officer on the hook. "Well, thank you anyway. But please keep me informed if there are any developments. I still think this kid is a danger. And let me know about the cat food."

"Will do."

"Bye."

"Bye."

A few minutes later his phone rang. Hal Koch from chemistry. "I got your results, T."

"Wow. That was fast, Hal. And not a moment too soon. The police department is dragging its feet."

"Well, it wasn't too hard to identify. Sodium hydroxide. I'm afraid that poor animal had a very painful death. The chemical is common and cheap. We have it right here in our labs. We use it for acid-base reactions."

T was certainly familiar with sodium hydroxide, but he knew their small biology supply was out. He thought for a moment. "Any way to tell if some is missing?"

"No, not unless someone were to take a lot of it. We buy it in five-pound jars. It didn't take much to do the cat in."

"Thanks, Hal. You've helped me a great deal."

T recalled from Faye that Bradley Maun was taking chemistry.

Hal would be teaching the lecture for that course. He picked up the phone again. "Hal? T here. Just one more thing. You have a kid named Bradley Maun in your intro course?"

"Yeah. Quiet kid. Doing C work."

"Have you used sodium hydroxide this semester?"

Hal was the quickest of studies. "You don't think…?"

"I'm not sure what I think, Hal. But you've done your bit for national defense. Thanks again."

When it rained it poured. No sooner had T spoken with Hal than an email appeared in his inbox. From the provost. It was clearly in response to his message about the cat.

Where is your proof?

T leaned back in his chair and stared at the message. He felt his ire rising. He had no intention of responding in anger, or in any tone that could be construed as irrational. The clock on the wall of his office was one of those large-face affairs that ticked audibly until the minute hand jerked forward with an even louder "tock." T watched the clock for two long minutes, meditating on the wonder of the technology involved in making a device that was so constant and reliable. Then he returned to his computer and typed out his response.

Why are you so intent on protecting this boy?

He closed his laptop and turned his attention to the meeting with Clive and Boats. *Oh, you're gonna love this, brother.* That's what Clive had said. Well, good then. He needed something to love. Something that would perhaps be of value to him in his effort to…what? Keep his job? Salvage his reputation? Inflict harm on the administration for inflicting harm on him?

T worked long into the afternoon. He refused to look at his computer again for fear of getting entangled in a back-and-forth with the provost, which would be a distraction at a moment when he wanted to focus on his upcoming meeting. And then, a rising fear: he hadn't thought about Olivia lately. How was such a thing possible? Could it be that the present mire he was in was displacing thoughts about the thing closest to his heart? He recalled once advising a student who was considering medical school but couldn't commit to the idea. "What is giving you pause?" he had asked. The student said that he feared the demands of med school would mean his giving up all the things he had come to love: music, rock climbing, fishing. T remembered his response, which he had uttered with great conviction: "On the contrary. If you go to med school you must cling to the things you love; otherwise, your medical education will swallow you whole and you'll become the kind of doctor you don't want to be." T took out his wallet and looked at the picture of Olivia he kept there. It showed her in profile on a winter's day, snowflakes adorning her hair like stars. And he resolved that whatever the involvement to come, he would not allow it to swallow him whole.

T made a pit stop at home to check on Tootsie—she was safe and sound—before changing into his jeans and a nice winter sweater Olivia had knit for him. As he left the house he paused on the porch and threw furtive glances all around. But nothing seemed out of the ordinary.

He was the first to arrive at the Lotus. Again, the lounge was sparsely populated, dimly lit. An Abba tune—"Dancing Queen"—was being softly piped in. A middle-aged couple was seated at the bar. The woman was attractive, with pointed features and a sincere smile. Her companion was looking at her with a gentle intensity as if he couldn't quite believe what he was seeing. T took out his phone and, against his better judgment, checked his email. Nothing from the provost. Good. But there was a message from Magda. *Hey, long time. A penny for your thoughts?*

Funny. He had not been thinking of Magda lately. She had, like an ebbing tide, receded from heart and mind. As with the unsettling realization that he had neglected thoughts of Olivia, he wondered if this was a symptom of his self-absorption, or maybe something deeper regarding his sense of where their relationship was going. He pecked out a response. *Sorry. There have been developments. Let's connect soon.* It wasn't until he hit SEND that he considered how curt that response was. Just as he was about to send a more considerate amendment, Clive and Boats showed up. Clive was disheveled as usual, and Boats didn't look like much of an improvement since T had run into him on campus. His expression was still hangdog. "Hey, Boats. How's it going?"

Clive and Boats sat next to each other, opposite T. The French instructor heaved a sigh as he dropped his bulk into place. "Oh, making it," he said. "Working on my self-esteem."

Clive threw an arm around Boats and shook him vigorously as if he could rattle the mopiness out of him. "Oh, you'll make it!" he sang. "You always do."

Sheesh, thought T. Maybe Magda and Clive would make a good match. They could compete to see whose sun shone the brightest.

Boats shrugged and mustered an unattractive, self-pitying smile. "Yeah, I guess. Like I said, I just have to work on my self-esteem."

Clive signaled to the waitress. "Honey, over here!" The young, blond woman had the *Can do!* manner of a university student. "Clive," said T in a harsh whisper, "cut out the 'honey' stuff. She might be one of ours."

Clive pressed a hand to his mouth. "Oops." When the woman arrived he struck a more businesslike tone. "Wild Turkey on the rocks for me, and..." he turned to Boats. "What kind of a man's drink does our sea captain want? Yo-ho-ho and a bottle of rum?" Clive clapped his hands as if that was the cleverest thing anyone had ever said.

"I'll take a rum and Coke," said Boats, mournfully, as if he were asking for hemlock.

Clive turned to the waitress. "And a seltzer with a twist of lemon for the odd man out." Turning to T, "So Boats here could use some cheering up," he continued without preamble. Then he looked at their sullen colleague. "Boats, you're among friends here. So let us help you. It's what colleagues do. I don't mind getting the ball rolling. You had a tragic break-up with Nan."

T was mortified and couldn't help reddening. Clive was running the conversation like a talk show host, but T didn't know what he could do about it. Maybe this was part of his lawyerly shtick.

The waitress brought the drinks and placed them all around. "And bring a vodka Collins for my friend. He'll need something to chase that rum down the hatch." He looked at T and winked. "So tell us,

Boats. We're here to listen."

The French professor lifted his rum and Coke and took a hearty quaff. "Well, yeah, I had so much self-esteem with her. She helped me so much." He took another broad sip.

T broke in. "Boats, forgive me for being blunt, but you make it sound like you were one of her clients."

Boats waved a hand. "No, no, it wasn't like that at all. She was my girlfriend. We had good times together." The man's eyes were growing moist. T found himself willing those tears to stay within their bounds. He did not want to have to comfort a crying colleague. "Sorry for interrupting, Boats. Just continue your story." Clive looked at T, then closed his eyes, firmed his lip, and nodded approvingly.

Another swig of the rum and Coke, and then another, and another, until the glass was empty. As if on cue, the waitress arrived with the vodka Collins. "Here's your chaser!" sang Clive as he took the drink and shoved it in front of Boats, who immediately seized it and brought it to his lips. "Like I said, I felt so much self-esteem with her, like I really mattered."

It occurred to T that if Boats said "self-esteem" one more time he would scream. "Boats, you don't need another person to validate your self-worth." As he said this, he wondered to what extent Olivia might have validated his. Was it possible that he was something less without her?

"It was just this huge distraction," said Boats. "This thing I had to constantly crawl over, or around, or under, to reach her."

T and Clive exchanged glances. "Explain," said Clive.

"She became obsessed with this...this student, like it was her life's work."

Clive prompted him. "What student?"

"This boy, this Bradley something or other."

T shuddered, then leaned across the table, as if he could crawl inside Boats's thoughts. "Bradley Maun?"

Boats brightened. "Yeah, that's the one."

T pressed on. "When you say 'obsessed,' do you mean, er, sexually?"

Boats waved T off. "Oh, no, nothing like that. I think she was afraid of him. She thought…"—he hoisted the vodka Collins—"… she thought that she was the only one standing between this kid and some kind of catastrophe." Boats was beginning to slur his words, and it didn't escape T's notice that the French professor had pronounced 'catastrophe' as 'catas*troph*.'

All three men took a breath. The waitress came over. "You guys doing okay?"

Clive nodded and sent her on her way. "Go on, Boats. You're doing good." As the man attempted to lift his drink again, Clive took his hand and lowered it to the table. "Ease off for a bit, will ya? Just tell us what went on."

Boats became dreamy as if he were entering a trance. "She… she had this idea that she could reach him. She said that he was dangerous but that she understood him. Said he could easily be an arsonist or shoot up a school, that's how near the edge he was." He gave a little laugh. "She even talked about getting a gun to defend herself. Just in case."

Clive noised, "Did she?"

"No. When I asked her why she didn't get the gun she said she was afraid she might use it on him."

T's head was reeling. By turns, he felt relieved, frightened, elated, and, in the last analysis, sorry for Boats. For all the man's credentials, there was something simple-minded about him.

Clive: "Go on, Boats. How did Nan think she could help him?"

Boats eyed his drink and licked his lips. He glanced at Clive as if seeking his permission. Clive put up one finger and nodded. Boats took his sip and sighed. "If Nan knew I was telling you all this she'd have a cow."

Clive laughed convivially. "You're doing great."

T was still leaning across the table. He lowered his voice to a near-whisper. "How did she think she could help a kid with such deep problems?"

Boats's expression clarified. He looked directly at T. "Kid? What do you mean, 'kid'? He's twenty-six years old."

Twenty-six? Bradley Maun's smooth moon face and big, childlike eyes could have allowed him to pass for a sixteen-year-old. They were not dealing with an impulsive adolescent, then. T pressed his question.

"She had this theory about the brain. Hidden places. Locked-up potential. She thought she could help him get into those places in his brain and release the goodness. Or something like that."

"Dr. Jekyll and Mr. Hyde," said T, and he looked at Clive, whose gaze was fixed on Boats.

"I think that's when things got to the point of no return with us. She had Bradley over the house for dinner. It was a real nice dinner, with candles and everything. She thought that if Bradley could see how normal people live it would give him something to strive for, put him in a frame of mind to unlock his brainpower, take control, and improve himself."

T looked on in great discomfort as Boats shed the first of his tears, which rolled down his cheek, made its way to the tip of his chin and plopped into his drink. But he felt obligated to keep the conversation going, lest the momentum be lost. "How did the dinner go?"

Boats's tears gave way to gentle laughter. "I went to the bathroom and Nan got up to get some salad dressing. When she got back he… he had lit the tablecloth on fire with one of the candles. The thing really went up. Nan flipped. I came back in when she grabbed the tureen of potato soup and doused the flames with it."

T took a deep breath and sat back. "Jesus Christ. What was Bradley doing while this was going on?"

Boats wiped his face with his napkin. "He was just sitting there, like a kid who wasn't getting a cake for his birthday. His face looked just sort of sad."

Clive: "What did Nan think about all this?"

Boats put his hand around the vodka Collins but made no move to lift the glass. "She lost it on him, screaming like I never saw her scream before. Called him a psychopath. But it didn't matter. He just looked into the distance with this blank expression, like he had been photoshopped into a picture of the dining room. Like he didn't really belong there. Then Nan pulled herself together and apologized to him. Get it? *She* apologized to *him*. As if it mattered. He couldn't tell the difference between an apology and if she had hit him in the head with a two-by-four. It was all the same. Just this dead, dead, dead look in his eyes. We took him home. Nan didn't want to be alone with him because she was afraid he'd grab the steering wheel and drive the car off the road. When we got back she read me the riot act. Said I couldn't say anything about what had happened. I told her someone had to call the cops. That's when she said she didn't love me anymore."

"That was precipitous," said T.

Boats nodded and looked over at Clive, who nodded in return. Both men watched as Boats drained his glass, which he then held up as a signal to the waitress. Clive took the glass from his hand. "You've had enough, Boats."

The look of loss in his eyes was pathetic. "Enough?"

Clive nodded, his face flush with sympathy for a man who had performed above and beyond the call of duty.

Boats looked from Clive to T and then down at his hands. "I don't know why I told you all this."

"Well," said Clive, "you had to tell someone. You couldn't keep it all bottled up. If you can't tell your friends, who can you tell? I hope you feel a little better now."

Boats shrugged. "I feel sleepy."

T was still processing all the new input. Nan had apparently known for a while how volatile Bradley Maun was, but she had kept it to herself, putting everyone in danger. And the chapter wasn't over yet. Bradley was still at large, still haunting T, still a student at Skowhegan College.

"Well, this looks like a merry band."

T had never seen Faye outside the campus. She had come over to the table, smiling. T felt strangely off-balance. He regrouped, indicating the empty chair next to him. "Care to sit? You know Clive and Bo…er Ted?"

Faye assented. "I have a few minutes. I ordered take-out for me and my son." She settled into the seat and looked from face to face. "I don't think we've ever spoken. But I know your names. I'm Faye.

Adjunct in chemistry."

"Welcome to our noble gathering," said Clive.

Faye smiled. "Ah, nobility. What good company."

T was still looking her over. Her relaxed demeanor and familiar manner made her fit right in. "I didn't know you had a son."

Faye bit her lip. "That's because the only thing we ever talk about is agar and slime molds. Yes, I have a life outside the lab. My boy Aidan is seven."

"Aidan," echoed Boats. "I just love that name. I once had a dog named Aidan."

"Ah, gee, Boats." T was shaking his head.

Faye laughed. "It's okay. I'm honored. Or my son is honored. Or someone is honored. In any case, Ted, I know what you meant."

Boats looked at Faye with appreciative eyes.

The four fell into friendly conversation about more mundane doings at the college. Clive told a story about a forgetful colleague who showed up in an empty classroom and then insisted that the absent students be disciplined. Then he realized it was he who was in the wrong room. Faye howled at that one. She grabbed T's arm as if for support. At that moment another face appeared in the lounge. Magda Zweck was staring at the festive four, but her gaze soon settled on T, whose arm was still hooked by Faye Mundy. When their eyes met, there was an exchange of subliminal information. T managed to raise his hand, signaling to Magda to come over. She turned and left the restaurant. T looked out the window and watched as she hurried to her parked car.

Faye turned out to be quite the conversationalist. She could have been an interviewing journalist, showing an intense interest in each person who spoke. When Boats mentioned his sailing activities, she brightened. "My husband tried to teach me to sail, but that was long ago and I've forgotten most of what I learned. The only thing I remember is to duck when someone says 'Come about.'"

Boats nodded approvingly. "That's the most important thing."

"What does your husband do?" asked T.

"Oh, not much of anything since he died."

No one said, "I'm sorry." In lieu of this, T reached out and patted Faye's hand.

A young man came over with a paper bag and handed it to Faye. "Ah, General Tso's chicken."

Clive indulged in a mock salute. "Long may he wave." Boats raised his empty glass. "To the general!" Both men looked imploringly at T, who excused himself with, "I'm not a military man."

They all watched as Faye, clutching the bag to her chest, left the table. "See you guys around the shop."

"Well," said Clive, "that was a nice interlude." And then to T: "You dog. I saw the way she looked at you. The way she took your arm."

T raised his seltzer. When he tilted the glass to drink, the lemon wedge dislodged and the water splashed down his neck. "Ah, gee..."

Clive turned to Boats. "See the irony? He doesn't drink alcohol, and yet he has a drinking problem."

The three shook hands. "We'll be in touch," said Clive. "We have to do this more often. I like you guys."

"Thanks for listening," said Boats.

T nodded. "Thanks for telling. I hope things smooth out for you."

"The seas were rough for a while, but now I have calm winds. I feel more self-esteem, especially after talking to you guys."

T gritted his teeth. He put "self-esteem" in the same refuse bin with "rubric," "paradigm," and "learning outcomes"—language that academics used to sound schooled.

Clive turned to Boats. "I'll take you home. And I'll pick you up in the morning so we can come back for your car."

Boats was on his feet. "I can drive." He swayed against the table.

"That's what they all say. Come on."

As the two men left the table Clive turned one last time to T. He mouthed one word in exaggerated fashion.

Goldmine.

TWENTY-THREE

She knew. Damn it, she knew. This thought pursued T through a sleepless night.

And still, life went on. Everything looked normal. T was teaching his classes, advising students, thinking of books he'd like to read, and occasionally meeting up with colleagues. It occurred to him, however, that he hadn't been writing. Until a short while ago he had disciplined himself to write one page of clean prose every morning, before leaving for school. If he didn't, he would fret the rest of the day about not having time to get to the task. But what to write? All of his essays to date had been about some aspect of natural history. Perhaps he should address something else he knew well. Teaching? God knew he had enough material for a book. Would a volume of teaching essays work?

This was the thought that competed for attention as T, still tired, made his way across campus under somber, roving skies. October was advancing and the grounds were decorated with pumpkins and corn sheaves bound to the railings fronting some of the older buildings. It was chilly, but not yet cold. That would come later, along with driving snowstorms. As T passed in front of the union, he spotted Praveen Khatri coming through the front door. The man brightened when he saw T. "It's been a while since we've spoken."

"Yes, I'm sorry about that. You're certainly one of the people I don't want to neglect. I think I can tell you that there has been a dramatic development."

"Dramatic?"

"Yes. Praveen. The college has threatened to terminate me. I guess you can say they have decided to terminate me, effective the end of this semester."

The mathematician looked pained. "I am shocked. They cannot do that. You have tenure."

"Well, we shall see. I'm certainly not going to simply walk away. Not after forty years." He smiled. "It just struck me that when I started teaching here, the provost was still in elementary school, making cut-outs of jack-o-lanterns."

Praveen took T's arm. "I will not abandon you."

T was struck by his choice of the word "abandon." Of all things. "Well, there's not much you can do. I appreciate your friendship."

Praveen was nodding, harboring a look of intense consternation. "You might be surprised at what I can do." And then, "Is all this about the trigger warnings?"

"Basically."

"I see." He brought a hand to his chin. "I see what I must do."

T felt the most compelling urge to reach out and hug this dear little man. "Don't worry too much about me."

Praveen's eyes widened. "I can't think of a better way to spend my time. Do you agree?"

"The sentiment means a lot to me."

The men parted and T continued on to his office. As soon as he took off his coat and put his laptop on his desk his phone rang. It was that very systematic officer from the police department. T had all but forgotten about their involvement. "Yes?"

"Professor Tarnaszewski, we have a report from the crime lab."

"Yes?"

"The chemical in the cat food was sodium hydroxide."

"Yes, I independently confirmed that."

There was a momentary silence at the other end of the line as if T had upended protocol and the man now needed to recalibrate. "So what now? I tell you I'm sure it was Bradley Maun."

"We questioned the young man, sir. He denied everything. But if you feel strongly about this you should keep us informed. The incident is now a matter of record."

T hung up. Then he called animal control and told them there was no longer a need to hang onto poor Benno.

T checked his email. He expected to see something from Magda. Nothing. But Clive was checking in. His message was cryptic.

> *All of our future communications relevant to the issue should be by voice or in person. Let's meet later in the day. Your office? Four o'clock?*

It was hard to believe that such a somber, no-nonsense email emanated from the festive, joking Clive. T immediately sent his own minimalist reply: *Okay.* In truth, he was desperately interested in hearing Clive's take on the previous night's confessional with Boats.

T did some revisions on his lab handout and then headed for class. The operative question had become, *Would Bradley Maun be there today?* As he approached the building he came across Magda walking the opposite way. She saw him but made no sign of acknowledgment. "Hey, you were at the Lotus last night. Why didn't you come over?"

Magda scrunched her shoulders together and looked around. "Oh, I saw that you were involved, so I didn't want to interrupt."

"You wouldn't have interrupted."

She looked up at him, her expression doubtful.

"Do you want to catch up sometime? There have been developments and I want to keep you in the loop."

Magda stomped the cold from her feet. "Sure. Sometime. I'll let you know."

And that was that. She continued on her way as T looked after her.

The students were already sitting in their places along the lab benches. A few were chatting, but most were on their devices, their minds elsewhere. Bradley Maun was present, seated by himself at the bench in the corner, staring blankly into the nothingness. He was in his standard uniform—black hooded bench warmer, unzipped, with a red-and-black plaid button-down shirt underneath. But there was a detail T couldn't tolerate. He was barefoot.

T gave the sheaf of lab handouts to a student and asked her to pass them around. He announced to the class, "Please read the introduction and we'll take it from there." Then he went over to Bradley Maun, who looked up and past him. He spoke in low tones. "Bradley, you can't be barefoot in lab. Do you understand why?"

He turned his eyes to T but they were sterile, vacant things that seemed to be looking through him. "Listen, we often break glassware in here and I can't guarantee that there are no shards on the floor. I just don't want you to get hurt. Where are your shoes?"

Bradley Maun swiveled away from T until he was facing the wall. At this point, the other students were tuned in and looking on. T excused himself. "Just give me a few minutes, please." He stepped into the hallway, took out his phone, and called Security. "Gary? T here. I have a situation." T explained the details and then returned to the lab, where he commenced the prep. Ten minutes later Gary Willins appeared. A no-nonsense, retired cop from the streets of Newark, his blackness was usually enough to warrant attention and cooperation, if only because he was a rare commodity on the almost all-white campus. T nicked his head in Bradley Maun's direction and Gary walked over to him. For his part, T continued the instruction. A moment later Gary interrupted him. "Sorry, Doc, but what is this stuff he's holding?"

T left the front of the room and walked a few steps toward Gary and Bradley. Then he stopped and squinted. "Bradley, please put it down."

Gary was still perplexed. "What is this bottle of stuff?"

"It's…it's hydrofluoric acid. Bradley, please put it down."

"Acid?" echoed Gary as he stepped back, his hands on his hips. "Dangerous stuff?"

T nodded.

Gary returned to Bradley. "Son, I don't know where you got that stuff, but your professor says it's dangerous. Can you please put it down so we can all get back to normal?"

Bradley seemed to be listening to Gary. He was at least looking at him with something resembling lucidity. And then, unceremoniously, he removed the stopper from the bottle.

"*Jesus H. Christ!*"

Gary was the first to move. Once Bradley began to pour the acid onto his foot both men were of a mind. T followed Gary in the rush to intercede. He got his hand on the bottle and wrestled it away while the security guard seized Bradley's other arm. "Get his foot to the sink, Gary."

While the rest of the class looked on, Gary hoisted Bradley out of his chair and sat him on top of a lab bench, lifting him under the arms like a child. T put the acid on a shelf, grabbed the student's foot and stuck it under a running tap. Bradley Maun offered no resistance. Gary held him firm nonetheless. T washed his foot with his hands, moving his fingers between the toes and under the sole and heel. The young skin was soft and uncalloused, but dirty, the nails broken and uneven. T felt a pulse of pity for him. After a good five minutes of rinsing, T lifted Bradley Maun's foot out of the sink and dried it off with paper towels. He examined the skin. It looked unaffected. "Bradley," he said, "you're lucky we got to you in time. That acid could have really burned you. Why would you do such a thing?" And then T caught himself. This wasn't the time or place for cross-examination. He nodded and then turned the student over to Gary, who took him by the arm and led him out of the lab.

The rest of the class looked on in silence as T moved to the front of the classroom with the bottle of acid in hand. He looked out at them and tried to strike a reassuring note. "Well, we all saw something today. I have to admit I don't understand what went on, but we should take this as a lesson in respect for these chemicals. I know I can count on you to take great care and wear your protective gear."

That was it. The lab progressed without further incident, but T was shaken. Bradley Maun was now threatening himself. Or was the acid incident simply another way to intimidate T? He just didn't know. *I'm not a psychiatrist, which is what this kid needs.* Of course, he couldn't—yet—suggest this to the volatile Nan Hays. Nan, who had apparently known all along that Bradley Maun was unpredictable and, yes, dangerous. *He lit her tablecloth on fire!*

The question lingered: How did Bradley get his hands on the acid? After class T inspected the adjoining prep lab. It didn't take Sherlock Holmes to figure out what had happened. The door to the acid locker was ajar. It had been a pretty bold move, entering a restricted space and seizing a dangerous substance. He must have done it while T was on the phone with Gary. When he got back to his office there was an email from the efficient security guard. Attached was an incident report. *Please fill in the details and I'll take it from there.* T completed the form in a very matter-of-fact manner, taking care not to include any value judgments or even educated guesses. Just the facts.

> *Bradley Maun came to class barefoot. He picked up a bottle of hydrofluoric acid and poured some on his foot. Chief of Security Gary Willins and I rinsed his foot. There was no evident damage. Gary then escorted Bradley Maun from the laboratory.*

T looked his statement over several times before hitting SEND. Then he called Security. "Hi, Gary. T here. I just filled out your report. Just curious about the resolution after you got him out of the classroom."

Gary whistled. "Wow. There was no resolution. That kid doesn't have much to say. I took him to the clinic for a look-see and they gave him an all-clear. Then I took him to Walmart and bought him a pair of sneakers."

"Where the hell were his own shoes?"

"Yeah, good question. I asked him but he didn't say squat. When I bought him the sneakers he put them things on without so much as a 'thank you kindly' and marched away."

"Yes, he's a marcher. So what happens now?"

"Well, I called Professor Zweck but she said this was a job for Professor Hays, so I called her and told her everything. It was curious."

"Why's that?"

"Well, she didn't get excited or anything. Just said she'd take it from there. Said I didn't even have to put in an incident report. But that's when I put my foot down. I told her, hey, it's not up to me.

If I don't put in that report then my ass is on the line. Although I didn't say it exactly like that."

"I appreciate your professionalism, Gary. It means a great deal to me."

"Hey, you did the right thing, cleaning that boy's foot and everything the way you did, like Jesus and his disciples. Not many professors would care like that. They would have called me and then stood back."

"Thanks, Gary."

T opened his M file and updated it, including Gary's comment that Nan Hays did not want an incident report. And then, just in case, T copied the file to a thumb drive, which he attached to his keychain.

So what now? The incident report would filter up the line, all the way to the president. In the interim, T had an unpredictable student on his hands. Instead of hurting himself, Bradley Maun could have slung the acid at him, or another student. No, it was insane to allow him back into class. T drafted an email, addressed to the Provost, Dean Olib, Nan, and the president.

> *If you haven't already, you will soon be seeing an incident report regarding student Bradley Maun. He deliberately mishandled a dangerous acid in class today. There were no injuries, but the potential for a serious outcome was great. In light of the unpredictable behavior of this student in an environment in which we work with glassware, open flames, and flammable and corrosive substances, I cannot allow Bradley Maun to return to my class. I hope you see that it is a question of student safety and liability.*

T knew that the operative word was "liability." He took pains to put it at the end of his statement, where it would have the most impact. Institutions were always worried about liability. If Bradley Maun wasn't a risk to the general well-being of the school's community, then nothing was.

T spent the next two hours plowing his way through a thick pile of student lab reports, but his mind kept wandering. Gary had called Magda. Strange that she hadn't contacted T to ask if he was okay. She was incubating something, and T was convinced he knew what it was. Just as he was ruminating, there was a knock. T gave a start and jumped to his feet. The door opened a crack. "Sorry. I didn't mean to take you by surprise."

"No, no problem. I'm just a little on edge."

Faye Mundy came into his office. "I heard about what happened in your lab today."

T indicated a seat. "I'm afraid I'm getting a reputation as an incompetent. Every day seems to bring a new crisis. How did you find out?"

"Some of your students are also in my chem lab. If it's any consolation, they view you as a hero."

"An overworked word," said T. "These days it seems that anyone who manages to get out of bed in the morning is hailed as a hero."

Faye smiled warmly. "I like cynicism when it's self-effacing."

T returned her smile. "I do appreciate your concern. I've told the administration that I don't want Bradley Maun back in class."

"Good for you. I'm behind you one hundred percent."

T immediately realized how bold and risky that sentiment was. Adjuncts had no protections and generally made it a practice not to get involved in any "issues." As such, they were adept at keeping their heads down and overworking for their miserably low pay. "Just hearing you say that means a lot to me. The really hard part about all this business is feeling so alone."

Faye was focused on him, her empathy palpable. "You're not alone. You have more friends than you think."

"Do you know something I don't know?"

"Perhaps. Just keep doing what you're doing."

"If the administration learns that you're supporting me they won't be kind to you."

Faye leaned toward him and took his hand. "Look, I worked on a flight deck in the Navy. Then I was a guard in a military prison. I've dealt with tougher characters and come out of it in one piece. Plus, I'm raising a son on my own."

T squeezed her hand. Why had it taken so long for him to get to know Faye? She was brassy. He liked that. "Appreciate it."

Faye got up. "Back to the races." And then, "Stick to your guns.

At least you'll know you're alive."

T realized there was a difference between saying, "Go get 'em," and "Let's go get 'em." Would Faye follow through and stand by him? He had no right to expect this. He needed to be prepared to go the distance solo. If someone else did leap into the fray, good, but he wasn't going to count on it.

Four o'clock drew up. To his credit, Clive appeared right on time. He was red-faced and huffing. "Is the elevator still out of order?"

"Yes," said Clive as he pulled up a chair. "But no worries. I need the exercise." He wheezed and coughed.

"Yeah, but not at the price of a heart attack."

Clive waved him off. "Well, that was some meeting with Boats. He's our Deep Throat."

"Yes, it bowled me over. What does Nan think she's accomplishing by shielding this student and making excuses for him?"

"I'm with you, brother. Let's take a breath and talk about next steps."

T nodded. "I can't believe Nan knew about this student. How dangerous he was. I mean, starting a fire in her house!"

"Let's not ignore the most important question. To wit: did the administration know? Or did Nan keep it to herself?"

"Either way…"

"No, no, no. No 'either way.' This is a critical question. It's *the* critical question. If the higher-ups knew and put you and our students at risk…"

T held up a hand. He then went on to explain the acid incident. When he was done, Clive looked apoplectic. "My God, my God. The plot thickens. This is the period at the end of the page. The kid is a danger and he's still in school."

"Clive, I don't want to hurt this student. He's troubled."

"Of course we're not going to hurt this student. Bradley Maun is a red herring, albeit a complicated one. We have to focus on what the provost, the dean, or the president knew. If you, and the students, were in danger…"

The desk phone rang. T looked at the read-out. "Ah, shit," he said. "Graveline."

Clive became animated and mouthed *Take it.*

T answered. He listened, and hummed. "I had no idea. I'll chat with him. Goodbye." He hung up and turned to Clive. "I don't know if this is good or bad. The provost said that Praveen Khatri is sitting outside his office and won't leave. It's some sort of protest. For my benefit."

Clive smiled and scratched his head. "Khatri? I didn't think he had it in him." And then, "What does the provost want you to do?"

"He thinks I put him there. He wants me to recall him."

Clive threw T a curious look. "Did you put him there?"

"Of course not."

"Then leave him alone. He's old enough to be your father."

TWENTY-FOUR

A PLAN. THAT'S WHAT Clive and T agreed they needed before Clive left T's office. A plan. And then he checked his watch and hurried off to his class.

The provost called again. "I'm glad you're still in your office."

"This is where I work. For a little longer, at least."

T heard the provost's heavy sigh of exasperation. "Don't get snippy," he scolded as if talking to a five-year-old. "I'm calling because I'm looking at this incident report."

T was feeling mischievous. "What about Professor Khatri?"

"He's still here. I told you to retrieve him."

"What about the incident report?"

The provost did not appreciate being whiplashed. "Listen now, I have some questions."

"All right."

"What were you doing with this, this hydro-flooric—is that the pronunciation?—acid in the classroom? It's an acid, so it must be dangerous."

T recalled that the provost's field was Hospitality Management. "Not all acids are dangerous. Vinegar is an acid. But yes, this one is. To answer your question, Provost, it was not in the classroom. Apparently, Bradley Maun entered the prep lab—bypassing the sign that says 'Authorized Personnel Only'—and took it out of the acid locker."

"Hmm…acid locker. Locker. Was it locked?"

"We don't generally lock the acid locker. But I guess we'll have to start."

"Whoa, whoa. You don't lock it? So it was an open invitation to someone to create mischief."

T recognized the attempt at jujitsu. "Mischief? He poured the acid on his foot. He could have been severely burned. That's more than mischief." And then, "Wait. You're trying to make this about *me*?"

"The student had easy access to a place that should have been locked. What I see here is negligence."

"Then you must mean negligent use of a dangerous substance."

"No. I mean lax security. You all but put the acid in his hands."

T had had enough. "Provost, I see the game you're trying to play. I also know more about this student than you might suspect. And I know who else knows."

He could feel the provost seething through the line. "This will not go well for you."

"This conversation is over. You have the incident report. Please be advised that I have retained a lawyer. Goodbye."

T slammed the receiver down. He brought a hand to his forehead. Why had he said that last bit? He and Clive were in cahoots, but did they have a formal arrangement? When push came to shove, would Clive really be willing to go up against the formidable legal resources of the college? Goddamn it. He was uncomfortable admitting it, but he needed that second opinion, that second voice that was Clive. The potential for errors and self-infliction of wounds was too great to go it alone. Clive had already uttered the word "represent." Did he mean it? Yes, yes he did. T was convinced of it. He had to take the leap of faith and invest fully in Clive. With this in mind, he called his cell. Clive picked up on the second ring. "I think I may have made a misstep." Then he explained.

Clive sighed. "Yeah, you're right. It was a misstep. Let's not put the cart before the horse. I need you to trust my judgment and my experience. The last thing we want is to be in a hurry."

"I know. But the clock is ticking for me. Come December thirty-first…"

"Keep the faith, T. I'm on your side. From now on, refer all procedural and legal questions to me. You can be assured that they're writing down everything you say, so be careful."

T had papers to correct, classes to teach, students to advise. Yet here he was, fighting for his reputation and his career. At this stage of the game, at his age. Should he be fighting? He could have retired years ago. And still he persisted. Despite the ebbing quality of the students, the increasing inanity of the administration, and all the recurring intrigues that characterized the academy, he persisted. There were those moments when he was trying, for the love of God, to get a student to correctly spell "nucleus," and he wondered if he needed a Ph.D. for this. But further, he asked himself, in those same moments so riddled with doubt, if he was happy. And as if on cue, another student would write a note of appreciation or, in the case of a course evaluation, that comment for the ages he had once received—*Professor T is God.* T realized he had no right to expect gratitude, or even appreciation. It was, after all, a job for which he was being fairly compensated. But yes, in the final analysis, he loved it. Science had always been in his bones—he had gotten his first chemistry set when he was seven—and it still was. He so enjoyed communicating it, attempting to make its arcana comprehensible. So he concluded that, aside from the current imbroglio with Bradley Maun, he was happy. This teaching business was what he was meant to do, what he was good at. To simply bow out because he was being told to leave was unthinkable. If Clive was willing to go to war on his behalf the least he could do was fight for himself.

T picked up the phone and called Magda. If nothing else, he needed to clear the air, to reduce the number of issues he was dealing with. Two rings. "Hey, it's me."

"Who's me?"

"Come on. I need to talk to you."

"Need?"

This was precisely the kind of banter T had no patience for. The older he got the more he needed communication to be in braille.

"Look," he said, "I'm going for broke here. You're disgusted with me. Can we agree on that?"

Magda sighed. "Oh, T…we're in the thick of the semester and I've got a line of students outside my door…"

"Really? A line?" He tried to keep his tone light and playful, but he knew that in this rarefied atmosphere of veiled feelings he was failing.

"T, please don't cross-examine me."

"It's just that I thought you were interested in my situation." How sad, how very sad this made him sound. "Can't we just meet and talk?" He could *feel* her checking the clock in her office.

"I'll be walking over to the union soon. If you want, you can walk with me."

She made it sound as if she were dispensing a privilege. "Yes, okay. I'll come by your building in, what? An hour?"

"That'll be fine."

T realized that nothing, at the moment, was "fine." He wasn't even sure what he would say to Magda. The words had a habit of coming when needed, though. And so, an hour later, he was standing in front of the counseling center, watching the students hustle about. Those who knew him paid generous regard. Some came over to chat. T had long felt that if he could get paid for simply interacting with the students, listening to their stories, and encouraging them without having to grade them, life would be heaven. In the middle of this rumination, Magda appeared. She didn't even pause in her movements but walked past him toward the union. T stepped lively to catch up with her. "So?"

"So."

T laid a hand on her arm to detain her. Magda stopped and threw him a blank glance. "Please," said T, retaining his hand on her arm. "This isn't an assault or a microaggression. I'll talk fast because I know you're in a hurry. The college is dumping me. By the end of the semester, I'll be gone. Clive is a lawyer. Maybe you didn't know that? He's helping me out. In the meantime, we've learned a great deal about Bradley Maun. He's dangerous. And Nan knew. Yesterday, in class, he poured acid on his foot. The provost is blaming me for the incident."

T took a breath and searched Magda's face, her eyes, for evidence of engagement. There was nothing there. He took his hand from her arm. She asked, "Why are you telling me all this?"

That was it, then. She had disconnected. "I thought you were interested, that's all. I'll stop now. There will be a resolution, for better or worse, and I'm sure you'll hear of it by semester's end."

Magda resumed her trajectory for the union. T walked with her. "A few final words because I now have nothing to lose. You changed when you saw me at the Lotus with Clive, Boats, and Faye, who was not part of the meeting. She came in to pick up food for her and her son. Then she left."

"Is that it?" Magda was looking straight ahead, her pace accelerating.

"No. Two more things. Jealousy doesn't become you. And I don't believe that you hate me."

Magda stopped and turned a cold, desperate eye on T. "Hate? Why would I hate you?"

"Because, dear Magda, I would prefer it. Hatred is an honest emotion, something I could orient to. But it's not the opposite of love. The opposite of love is indifference."

She slowly shook her head. A small, glacial smile of disbelief broke. "Oh, you poor man. Whoever said that I loved you?"

T stood rigidly in place as Magda walked away. He kept looking after her, wondering if she would turn one last time, throwing him a glance to acknowledge that a pilot light of concern still flickered.

She didn't turn.

TWENTY-FIVE

It occurred to T that, except for the eighteen-year interval with Olivia, he had been lonely most of his life. As a child growing up in Boston, he had always strayed, alone, to the waste places, the margins: the reedy wetlands along the waterfront, the excavations for new roadways, the drainage ditches where, remarkably, minnows thrived. He didn't realize until he had moved to Maine to teach at Skowhegan, that what he had been longing for all along was space. Although he had profited from growing up in a city—it had endowed him with a good dose of street smarts—it came to not feel right. Those childhood wanderings by Boston Harbor had been a message, and he was glad he had heeded it. Maine turned out to be easy on the eyes and the spirit. More of an idea than a location on the map, it nonetheless had an "end of the road" feel that gave T a sense of place, and embrace. He was convinced that living in Maine had put him in the state of mind to be open to a person like Olivia, who had also sought refuge in Maine because she resonated with its landscape, its broad expanses of silence, its culture of sufficiency. He was grateful for the eighteen years he had had with her. And now he knew, at age sixty-five, that eighteen years was nothing, that in eighteen years he would probably be dead.

Curiously, these thoughts made it easier to accept Magda's apparent loss. Yes, he had, after that last encounter, quickly conceded that she was lost to him. And now events continued to pull him forward, inexorably. T knew that he had to pick his battles, and the one he was engaged in with Bradley Maun and the administration was enough for the moment. It seemed that every time he was in his office the provost tried to call. But T had ceased answering. A wise move? If the provost wanted to see him he could send an email, which, unlike a phone call, could be preserved as documentation. No sooner had T completed this thought than a message from the provost arrived that drove him to frantic distraction.

Bradley Maun said you deliberately broke glassware on the floor so he would cut himself. What was he doing barefoot in a biology laboratory? And why have you retained an attorney? Please answer your phone!

T's impulse was to open the torpedo doors, arm the weapon, and launch it. But he relented, mindful of his philosophy in such matters. He copied and pasted the email into his M file. The evidence was accumulating, the timeline growing. T went off to teach his intro bio lecture. Bradley Maun was, thankfully, absent. Had the administration heeded his insistence that this student be barred from his class? When T returned to his office, in a more collected frame of mind, he reopened the provost's message and replied.

Do you believe I deliberately broke glassware to injure a student? As for Bradley Maun's being barefoot, please ask him. And thank Gary Willins for his professionalism and his compassion in buying this student a pair of shoes.

T lingered over his reply for a few moments, reading it two or three times. Too harsh? Combative? Certainly oppositional. *Oh, hang it.* He hit SEND.

Clive checked in. "Aren't cell phones great?" he sang. "I can find you wherever you are."

"It's a curse."

"Now, now. We have work to do. How about the Lotus tonight?"

"I think we need a change of venue. The Lotus provides too much opportunity for mayhem."

"What are you talking about?"

"I'd be happier someplace else."

"Well, oookay, then. How about my place?"

Odd. He had never conceived of Clive as having a "place." The only context in which he knew him, outside the Lotus, was campus. "Where do you live?"

"The bitter end of South Penobscot Street. You can't miss it. Come at seven. That way I won't have to feed you. Ha!"

"I'll be there."

"Oh, and we may have company."

"Company? Who? Clive…?"

He had hung up. Oh, no, now T had something else to brood over. A thought flashed through his mind of entering Clive's home and—*bang!*—Bradley Maun would be sitting there, a bid on Clive's part to play peacemaker. Or maybe he had gotten wind of the rough waters with Magda and wanted to patch things up between them. Could either of these things be possible?

T wore out the day sitting at his desk, correcting papers. He considered again what a pleasure teaching would be if not for the conveyor belt of papers written in something purported to be English. T couldn't help smiling when he recalled the story of one of his English colleagues, Maria Silvestri, who had become so frustrated by her students' poor work that, one day, she stood before the class and told them, "Every time I leave this room I go to my office, close the door, lay my head down on my desk, and I just cry."

T knew better than to ever berate his students in such a cruel manner. He felt too much affection for them. But this bonhomie did not prevent him from remembering that, in the administration's eyes, the name of the game was "warm bodies," and Skowhegan College was adept at reeling them in. Nobody ever mentioned that the graduation rate at the school was an anemic eighteen percent. In Voldemortian fashion, it was the "statistic-that-must-not-be-named."

What was that crack Clive had made about not feeding him? Knowing Clive, it was no doubt true. T stopped at the house to check on Tootsie and then made a barebones tuna salad sandwich for himself. As he took a bite of the paltry meal, Tootsie hopped onto an adjoining chair, watching him with narrow eyes. For his part, T returned the feline's gaze and held the sandwich out to her. She sat up and pawed it to pieces before hopping down onto the floor and padding into the living room, leaving pawprints of mayonnaise on the tiles. "Oh, that's nice," said T as he got up. "Now neither of us will be eating it."

Before leaving the house, T opened the snail mail. Two bills, an early Christmas card from a relative in Poland, and a couple of unsolicited catalogs for gift baskets. But buried in the mire was a letter from the college. T immediately suspected it was not a holiday greeting.

Dear Professor Tarnaszewski:

Reflecting previous communications, this is to inform you that, as a result of your gross insubordination in not heeding the directives of the Provost's office, your employment with Skowhegan College will be terminated as of Dec. 31 of the current year.

I thank you for your service and wish you well in your future endeavors.

Sincerely,
Nedly Trumbull
President

T recalled Nan's memorable quote from a past college president: *An institution is incapable of showing gratitude.* Because he knew this to be true, he was, in a way, prepared for this moment. And he pitied those colleagues who believed that, if they only joined one more committee, advised one more student, got one more grant, took on one more course, wrote one more forgettable paper, the school would come to view them as indispensable. But the dirty little truth was that no one was indispensable. It was a cold calculus, but T had never seen any evidence that contradicted it.

He took the letter with him as he set out for Clive's place. It was Halloween eve, and the environment was conspiring to play its part. The full moon was periodically obscured by roving clouds, alternately shading and illuminating the cold, silent landscape. The wind was stiff and biting. T got into his car, blowing warm air through his hands and willing the heater to hurry up and do its job. He headed out into the night.

South Penobscot Street was at the edge of town, on the other side of the freight tracks where a pulp and paper mill, long gone, had once brought working-class prosperity. An unkind local legend was that children born to the families in that corner of town had six toes. The neighborhood was still known as "Crow Valley," but the moniker had become a badge of pride as university families moved in and spiffed up the properties. But enough of the old guard remained to give the place the ambience of a work in progress, or decay. According to local code, it was permissible to have up to three wrecked cars on one's front lawn, and several Crow Valley denizens pressed this guidance to its limit, if only out of defiance.

Clive's directions had been right on the mark. At the very end of South Penobscot was a small, careworn cape. In the solitary, flickering streetlamp T was able to make out a sickly yellow, clapboard affair with brown window trim. The front yard was overgrown with tall weeds. In the middle of the mire was one unpruned crabapple with crooked limbs, looking like a distressed mother looking for wayward children. There were three cars in the gravel driveway. *What is this? A convention?* T parked on the street, at the edge of the front yard.

From the doorstep, T could hear voices within. He knocked and Clive blossomed on the threshold. "T!"

"What a surprise, eh?"

Clive reached out and gathered T into the house. They passed through a cluttered mudroom heaped with shoes, boots, assorted tools, and a precarious load of poorly stacked firewood. Then they entered the kitchen, another disorderly scene replete with dishes piled in the sink, half-eaten food on the table, and torn-up linoleum. A bulldog reclined in the corner, ropey drool hanging from its jowls. "That's Primus," said Clive with pride.

"A good name for a bulldog. He looks like Winston Churchill."

"He does!" erupted Clive, as if the thought had never occurred to him.

They arrived in the heart of the house, a likewise cluttered living room full of curiosities, including a taxidermied salmon with an eye missing, the skull of a horse, a row of Hummel figurines, an open chessboard on a TV table, and a banjo. The room was dim and low-ceilinged, the furniture worn, but the woodstove was winking its yellow eye and exuding a cozy warmth. All of this paled when T confronted the "company" Clive had referred to. There, sitting in opposing easy chairs, were Praveen Khatri and Faye Mundy, who quipped, "Guess who's coming to dinner."

T wet his lips. "Clive said there would be no food."

"Oh, that's precious!" Clive sang as he clapped T on the back. "Actually, I have some *horse dovers*." T looked on as he produced a tray of unappetizing-looking snacks, all yellow, like the exterior of the house. "Sit down, T. On the sofa."

T shed his coat and sat. Turning to Praveen, "I'm surprised to see you here. I understand you held a sit-in for my benefit."

Praveen nodded, cupping a cracker and cheese in his hands. "The provost was not happy."

"I don't think it's easy to make him happy. Nevertheless, I thank you for your support."

"As you once said, I have nothing to lose."

T turned to Faye. "And what have we here?"

"I like living on the edge," said the adjunct.

"Where's your son?"

"With his favorite babysitter. I'm insanely jealous."

T smiled warmly. Clive took a seat with him on the sofa. He watched as T produced the letter from the president. "First things first. This arrived today." He handed the missive to Clive, who read it, grunted, and then passed it to Faye. "Good."

T's eyebrows took flight. "Good?"

"Yes," said Clive with a bounce. "Now we know exactly where we stand. This is a precious document. When push comes to shove they'll have to detail the reasons for the charge of insubordination."

"I don't like the word 'charge.' It makes this sound like a legal proceeding."

Clive slapped his leg. "You're prescient, T."

Praveen gave an audible "tsk" and handed the letter back to T. "This is unjust. Do you agree?"

"Praveen," said T, "I think that's the one thing we can agree on. But I'm very reluctant to drag you and Faye into this."

"Nobody's being dragged," said Faye.

Clive downed a cracker and cheese, followed by a swig of beer. "Nobody's being dragged," he echoed. "You need allies. If the administration knows that you have colleagues on your side, they are inclined to proceed with greater care."

T brooded for a moment. Looking up, "So we need a plan."

Clive darkened. He put down his beer and sat up. "T, what do you think is the central issue in all this, this mess?"

T shrugged. "I should be free to teach the truth as I know it without having to issue trigger warnings."

"Why?"

"Because it's a slippery slope. If they need a trigger warning for genetics, why not evolution, and immunotherapy, and..."

Clive put up a hand. "Not good enough. The slippery slope argument doesn't work anymore. Everyone uses it. It's been diluted."

T presented his palms. "So then?"

"So this. The provost is the chief academic officer. As such, he can demand trigger warnings..."

"So how does that help me?"

"I'm not done." Clive glanced from T to Faye to Praveen, confirming that he had everyone's attention. "Here's what you do. Don't try to push against an immovable object. Instead, use its weight against itself."

T was squinting. He wasn't used to hearing Clive speak in poetic terms. "Just give it to me straight. What do you want me to do?"

Clive raised his hand and flicked it as if trying to conjure something out of thin air. "We sue the college."

T sat back. He looked at Faye and Praveen, who seemed equally baffled. "Sue them? For what?"

"For not giving you a trigger warning."

"Again, for what?"

Clive leaned toward the middle of the room, his hands clasped. "For not telling you, warning you, about Bradley Maun. Damn it, man, I feel it in my bones that they knew, and they allowed a dangerous student, a threat, into your class. A kid who sets tablecloths on fire and deliberately mishandles industrial acids. You should have been given a trigger warning."

T took a couple of deep breaths. "My God. That's a hell of a strategy." And then, "I have three concerns, Clive. One, I don't want to target this student. Two, I don't want to hurt the college. And three, we don't know what the administration knew, or if they knew at all."

Clive nodded. "First, this is not a complaint against Bradley Maun. God knows the kid needs help. And don't worry about the college. Colleges retain lawyers, so they're well-armed. This is a shot across the bow. But it will get the trustees' attention. Let's see what happens then. As for your last point, yes, we have to find out what the higher-ups knew. I can't believe Nan Hays kept this to herself, considering how loose her lips were around Boats."

T scratched his head. "What, materially, are we suing for?"

Clive turned his eyes heavenward. "Let's say a million dollars. For mental anguish. And of course your reinstatement."

"That's vulgar. I mean, a million dollars. I don't want this to be about money. And don't quote Mencken to me."

"Money is just a device, a tool," said Clive, almost pleading. "Just to get their attention. Institutions fear only two things. Bad publicity and their pocketbook."

Faye spoke up. "T, it seems to me that the only alternative is for you to quietly leave, as requested. What would that accomplish? Would you be able to live with yourself?"

For some reason, T looked over at Praveen, who was regarding him with soft eyes. "Are you willing to put yourself at risk?"

"Yes. But I don't think it will come to that. Most mathematicians are not willing to take on my teaching load at my salary. They would have a hard time replacing me, and then there is the trouble of dislodging a tenured faculty member; I mean, for something other than insubordination. Moreover, I have been uncomplaining all these years."

"But in supporting me you're complaining now."

Praveen shrugged. "I have a lot of catching up to do."

T regarded Clive. "I appreciate everything you've done for me, but I'd still like to know why you're putting yourself on the line like this. Isn't there a conflict of interest? I mean, a lawyer filing suit against his own school?"

"Oh, you don't understand. I'm not suing. The union is suing. And they're just lucky enough to have an attorney willing to do the dirty work pro bono." Having said this, Clive looked around. "Everyone on board?" And then he settled his gaze on T. "Say the word and we'll man the ramparts. This is your battle. So what will it be?"

Faye was right. There was no easy way out that he could live with.

"Word."

With that, they adjourned.

TWENTY-SIX

THE SOMBER, CHILL DAYS of late October segued into an equivocal November. One day rain, the next overcast and threatening, and the next bright and promising. Then some light snow, followed by melting, followed by a hard frost. Such were the vagaries of the seasons in Maine. But all these climatic mood swings were premonitory. A mere overture. Soon the serious snow, and the cold, and coal-black skies winking with stars would put the decisive stamp of winter on the place, and they would settle in for the long haul.

For the moment, all was quiet. After the letter from the president, there had been no further communications from the administration, except for a brief email from the registrar announcing that Bradley Maun had withdrawn from Introductory Biology. This was a relief. T would no longer have to worry about whether the student would be in class, or whether he would pour acid on himself or wreak some other kind of mayhem. Of course, if everything continued on its present course, only eight weeks remained of T's career as a college professor, after which, what? Did one simply stop doing what had become second nature—the teaching, the lab preps, the grading, the advising, the faculty meetings? What would substitute for the rhythm he had established over the course of forty years?

Since the meeting at Clive's place, three days of silence had reigned. This was the thought that was crossing T's mind when his cell rang.

"This is huge!"

"What's huge?"

"I just talked to Boats. You won't believe this."

"Clive, just give it to me straight. Is it good or bad?"

Clive hummed. "Well, it depends on your point of view."

"Please…"

"Okay, brace yourself. Remember the reason Boats gave us for his break-up with Nan?"

T thought for a moment. "Something about his not being on board with her Bradley Maun concerns?"

"Essentially. Yes. But there was something he didn't mention."

"Do I have to drag it out of you?"

"She was carrying on with Larry Graveline."

"The provost?"

"The one and only."

T was dumbstruck. "My God."

"Say it again."

"My God." And then, "How did you find all this out?"

"I invited him to my house for supper last night."

"Supper? I thought you didn't serve food at your place."

Clive didn't miss a beat. "It was just mac and cheese. No big deal. But plenty of wine as well, to loosen his tongue."

"And?"

"And that's when he told me about Graveline. Can you believe it? Nan and Larry?"

T couldn't believe it. Nan was an attractive and, in her way, dynamic personality. What did she see in the stoop-shouldered, neckless, balding, obsessive provost with that crazy ring of red hair? "It just seems so unlikely."

Clive gave in to speculation. "Nan's a go-getter. Maybe she went and got him so she could go and get hers. He may not be much to look at, but he has power. Didn't someone say that power is the ultimate aphrodisiac?"

"In any case…"

"In any case, If Nan was so loose-lipped about Bradley Maun with Boats, who could do little to advance her career, I'm thinking that she opened the floodgates for the provost. He must have known everything about this kid."

"Okay, but why would he defend him and advocate for him, and try to turn the tables on me when Bradley Maun was the one who poured acid on himself?" And then, a light. "Wait. I think I see. Something to do with Nan's crazy brain theories."

Clive chortled. "You're in the groove, Jackson. If he didn't go along with her, no more nookie."

"This is all highly speculative."

"Yes. Highly. But all we need to do is show that the provost knew. And that he put you and your students at risk by allowing Bradley Maun to persist."

"So what do we do now?"

"You're still committed?"

"Of course."

"These things need to be handled by degrees. I'll draft a statement of intent to file suit, run it by the union, and present it to the administration. It's their turn to sweat."

"I don't want to make anybody sweat."

"Of course you do. Consider all the heartache and anxiety they've caused you. Bradley Maun. The dead cat. The acid. That letter of termination. Consider the moments when you felt most alone as if the world was coming down around you."

It struck T that Clive was already giving an oral argument before the court. But it was persuasive. "Okay. Do what you have to do. But again, Bradley Maun is not the target, and I don't want to impugn the school."

Clive concurred. "We're tightly focused here. It's about higher administration, not the school."

"What about Nan?"

"Listen, T. It's not the goal of a lawsuit to make everybody happy. It's an adversarial affair. Someone is going to be disappointed, to say the least. And there may even be a sacrificial lamb."

"I don't want to sacrifice Nan."

"Hey, I don't know how this whole thing will turn out. Who knows? Maybe you'll be the one whose head is dragged to the block."

TWENTY-SEVEN

When T got home that evening he fed Tootsie, made a salad for himself, and then sat down to write. He felt like a pianist who has been too long away from the ivories, staring at the keyboard, wondering if he still had it and what it would take to get back up to snuff. After a minute's pause, he began to type.

Whatever Happened to the Eccentric Professor?

T thought back on some of the oddball, but otherwise talented, professors he had had as an undergraduate at Princeton. There was Dr. Catavic, who was so forgetful that one day he went into the men's room with his briefcase and emerged with the toilet seat under his arm. And Professor Jaffee, who somehow managed to lose one shoe while teaching physics lab. He wound up shuffling around the room in a socked foot, mumbling, "Where is my shoe? Where is it?" And what was her name? Dr. Jenissee, who commuted in from another town but was frequently late for class because she kept confusing the New Jersey Turnpike with the Garden State Parkway.

Where did they go? What became of them? Which raised the question, where were the eccentrics today? An odd homogenization had taken place in the academy in the past twenty years or so, where the professoriate seemed to be of a mind, their meetings full of unanimity, nodding heads, an emphasis on "right thinking," and a malignant reluctance to rock the boat. Gone were the days when a man like Geoff Lamax—may he rest in peace—devoted research time to discerning the essence of the difference between Coke and Pepsi, and then triumphantly mounted the conference room table—in the middle of a faculty meeting!—to announce his findings. Or Tillie Margroff, whose research on the subject of nostalgia sometimes brought her to tears at those same meetings as she decried the superficiality and false promises of the modern day in favor of what she regarded as the more "genuine" culture of her favorite decade, the 1930s.

T had a theory. It lay in the way people used to be hired. Back then it was a matter of networking. The word would go out that someone was needed to teach, say, sociology. If you knew someone, you would recommend them and within a day or so the person would be on the job, idiosyncrasies and all. But today there was a hiring protocol, a sort of sieve, with many hands involved, from the president down to the department chair and Human Resources personnel. All were intent that the prospective hire be a good "institutional fit." In other words, they had to be team players who wouldn't be "difficult." Moreover, they had to pledge allegiance to the school's social creeds and agree to undergo various equity trainings, and so forth and so on. The result, again, was a blithering sameness with no prospect of hearing or seeing the unexpected. *The Stepford Wives* was the image that came to mind.

T caught himself. Perhaps he was being unfair. He considered that eccentricity had not disappeared from college campuses; it had simply migrated from faculty to administration: the colorful characters were now running the asylum. Exhibits A and B were the inscrutable, unblinking President Trumbull and the obsessive and vengeful philanderer, Lawrence Graveline.

But then, again, maybe T himself was the last of the old-time eccentrics. Was it possible that he was being pegged as such and that's the real reason he had to go?

It was in this frame of mind that he continued to write. As the words appeared on the laptop's screen he warmed to his subject and became conscious of his profound contentment with being in touch with the written word again. Olivia had once told him that he could be a successful full-time writer. Successful, perhaps, but socially isolated. Teaching was his way of being "out there" and meeting new and sometimes interesting people. And there was, of course, the occasional gifted student whose prospects T was in a position to promote.

And so he wrote, hour upon hour, deep into the night. Tootsie was curled up on a chair cushion, listening contentedly to the subdued clicks of the keyboard as if it were music to the feline ear. T's bliss swelled as well. He marveled anew at the power of words to evoke words, ideas to prompt ideas. With every keystroke, he felt as if he were dispelling the cloud of anxiety that had gathered above him since the beginning of the semester. When midnight struck he found himself with fifteen pages of text. He read his work, made some edits, and resolved that, come hell or high water, he would continue this project. That's when an oddly comforting thought occurred to him: if he did get the boot from Skowhegan, it might push him in another direction, toward the writing life, a door he had never fully opened. The trick was to write and still be in touch with people.

The ensuing days were sedate and uneventful. No Bradley Maun to grapple with, no word from Clive, and no contact with administration. Likewise, Magda was maintaining her silence and there was no sign of Boats. T mused that maybe Clive had succeeded in getting him into the Witness Protection Program. And what of Praveen Khatri? Had he returned to his vigil outside the provost's door? Probably not. He would have heard from Lawrence Graveline by now.

As T drove to school his thoughts jumped to Faye Mundy. Very much like Magda in some ways, but with an edge that Magda lacked. What was it that Faye had said about working on a flight deck and in a prison? Maybe she regarded T's preoccupations trivial by comparison. And yet, she had, at some risk to her position, invested herself in his cause.

T sat down at his desk and began to review his lecture notes. That's when Clive called. "Sorry for the radio silence over the past few days."

"I had begun to fantasize that this whole affair had gone away, or maybe it had been an illusion in the first place."

Clive huffed. "Fat chance. We're in it up to our necks. The union is behind our efforts one hundred percent. I sent the intent to file suit to the president the other day. From there it was no doubt forwarded upwards to the board of trustees and downwards to the provost. I'm surprised you haven't heard from him yet."

"Maybe he had a stroke when he saw it."

"Well, listen. And this is important. If anyone contacts you, refer them to me. Emotions are likely to be high, so you've got to remain calm and objective. Let them be the ones flying off the handle."

"Trumbull doesn't seem to be the type to fly off the handle."

"I'm thinking of the provost and Nan."

"How would Nan know what's going on?"

"Hey, your memory must be getting rusty. Remember what I told you about her being in bed with Graveline? We have to assume they talk freely to each other, perhaps in the heat of passion. But again, remember that you have representation. Use it."

T worked to dispel the image of a sexually passionate Lawrence Graveline. "And if the provost calls and rants?"

"You can listen to him all you want, but keep your mouth shut. Take careful notes, and take them immediately after the call, while your memory is fresh, especially if he makes any threats."

"Threats?"

"Yes. Remember what I said about emotions running high."

T wandered down to the prep lab to make sure everything was in order for the week's exercise. His heart rose when he spotted Faye, moving about in her white lab coat, a busy bee. "Hey, soldier."

She stopped and threw him a beguiling look. "Sailor," she corrected. "Remember? Flight deck?"

"Oh, yes. I never served."

She paused and put down a flask, then peeled off her rubber gloves. "I think what you're involved in qualifies as combat duty. So thank you for your service."

"Is there a medal for what I'm doing?"

"There should be. Considering what you're up against."

"You mean the students we teach?"

"I'm talking about the administration. T, I know institutions. They have a lot of resources, a lot of vested interests. I fear ours will come down on you with fury."

T gave her comment due consideration. "Should I beg off?"

Faye frowned. "You already know where I stand. No, you shouldn't beg off. The school put you in a terrible, and risky, and dangerous position. I just want you to steel yourself and lean on your friends."

"I guess I just need to be reminded now and then."

Faye sighed. "What are you doing tonight?"

"Aside from feeding the cat?"

"After you feed the cat."

T shrugged.

"Good. I'm picking up some food from the Lotus. Can you come over for a delicious supper?"

"Only if there's General Tso's chicken."

"Deal."

T watched as Faye resumed her prep and disappeared into the teaching classroom. He had no idea why his mind jumped to thoughts of Magda. She had clearly written him off. What message would he be sending if he contacted her now? Still, she had been an attentive and sympathetic ear. He didn't want to make believe she didn't exist. Maybe she was waiting for him to reach out again. He had grown to disdain ambiguity, but here he was, in the thick of it.

The day passed, and still no response from the administration. What if they didn't respond? No, they had to. A lawsuit was in the offing. They were probably strategizing, maybe waiting him out, hoping that he would go away as his termination date approached. He was becoming resentful of his preoccupation with the whole dirty business, resentful of the person he feared he was becoming, and resentful that he was becoming less mindful of Olivia over time.

When T got to Faye's he stopped short and stared. It was a small, gingerbread-house affair, with a sinuously curved front roof hip over an arched door painted powder blue. The whole of it was charming, set deep back from the road, shaded by ramrod-straight white pines. When Faye opened the door, light poured forth, spilling out onto the front step. The warm air that emanated was redolent with the smell of the General Tso's. "Brace yourself," said T as he stepped inside. "I'm going to compliment you on your home."

He handed her a bottle. "It's sparkling apple cider. I know you have a boy." He glanced about at the neatly appointed spaces, bereft of clutter, but with a toy here, a children's book there, to indicate that it was a home and not a museum. "It's a Sears house," said Faye as they walked to the kitchen. "They say it was built around 1933, in the heart of the Depression." Tillie Margroff would have approved.

There was an abundance of warm woodwork, set off from eggshell-white walls. The kitchen cabinets, however, were painted robin's-egg blue. "There's nothing Depression about it," said T. "It's lovely."

Faye busied herself with the food. "I just got in a little while ago myself. I had to pick up Aidan at after-school rec."

As if on cue, a child appeared in the kitchen. Stout, with short blond hair and striking green eyes, he stood there barefoot, smiling sweetly at T. "Aidan, this is Mr. . . ."

"Just T will do. I don't want him to confuse me with the character from 80s TV."

Aidan cocked his head. "What's 80s TV?"

"T is a biologist," said Faye as she brought a large serving tray to the already-set table.

"That's so cool," said Aidan. "Do you know anything about fungi?"

T smiled. "I know a lot about fungi."

"What about *Amanita muscaria*?"

T examined the boy's earnest eyes. "Fly agaric," he said. "It's not edible."

"But it's beautiful, isn't it?"

"Yes," said T. "And I guess that's the most important thing. It's beautiful. What more can we ask of it?"

The supper was congenial, with the conversation moving from weather to the winter ahead to favorite foods to Aidan's estimation of school (very cool, especially science). When the conversation momentarily brushed up against more serious topics, like public policy, Aidan didn't exhibit the least impatience. He either listened quietly or subdivided another chunk of chicken with competently wielded fork and knife. T found his eye wandering to the lad, this bright, pleasant, independent little human. A child had not been in the cards for him and Olivia, although the desire was there. They had attempted adoption but were daunted at every turn by bureaucracy. Over time, worn down, they abandoned the effort, and neither of them was the type to harbor regrets. But still…

"May I go to the bathroom?"

Faye nodded toward Aidan.

"Excuse me."

T watched as the boy left the room. "What a magical child." He realized he sounded like a Victorian uncle offering up his estimation of Little Lord Fauntleroy.

Faye smiled. "He has a good center. So far he's been easy to raise. No significant issues, no drama. We'll see what teenagerhood brings."

"He has two wonderful attributes."

"Oh?"

"He doesn't cling, and he doesn't whine."

Aidan re-entered the room and resumed his seat. "I was fast because I just had to pee. Do you know anything about *Amanita virosa*?"

"Sure do. It's the destroying angel, the most poisonous mushroom in Maine. I wouldn't even handle it."

"I got a mushroom-growing kit for my birthday. Do you want to see it?"

"Of course I do."

The boy took T by the hand and led him into the living room. "My gosh," said T, "you have a fainting couch."

Faye brought the back of her hand to her head. "I haven't had to use it yet."

T was struck by the room's coziness. Besides the red velvet fainting couch, there was a small conventional sofa, a Canadian glider, and a leather easy chair, all skirting the perimeter of an intricately detailed hooked rug. A few pillows and throws added an additional gloss, and to grace the entire scene, a woodstove pulsed in a corner, shedding a welcome warmth.

"Take a look."

T accompanied Aidan to the large window in the front wall's

build-out. There were several shelves with a variety of potted plants. A riot of mushrooms on long, slender stipes was growing from the side of a block of woody material. "It looks like the heads of the Hydra."

"They're oyster mushrooms," said Aidan, not grasping the allusion. "They started to grow three days after I got them." He picked up a spray bottle. "All you have to do is mist them a couple of times a day. Wanna try?"

T applied a couple of squirts. He realized that Aidan's curiosity and enthusiasm weren't singular. A lot of young kids rode hobby horses of intense interest. The question was, what happened by the time they got to college?

"Coffee?"

"Tea if you have it. Anything but Earl Grey. May I sit on the fainting couch? Or is it just for show?"

"Sit. Nothing here is off-limits."

T sat gently down. He ran his hands over the velvet. Aidan came over and took a place next to him. "We don't get a lot of guests."

"Well, you're the perfect host. I feel very welcome here. Tell me about your friends."

Aidan slipped his hands under his thighs and began to gently rock. "Oh, yeah. I have Daniel and Tyler and sometimes Jesse. None of them like fungi, so we usually ride bikes. I'm in rec soccer with Jesse."

Faye re-entered holding a tray. "How are the menfolk getting along?"

T looked down at Aidan. "How are we getting along, Sport?"

"Good." He looked the tray over. "The chocolate milk is for me. I don't like tea."

Faye sat in the easy chair, next to the woodstove. Aidan wandered over to a shelf and took out an oversized book titled *Railroads Across America*. He got down on the floor and opened it. "Do you like trains?"

"I love trains. I wish Maine had more of them."

There were a few more words about school, children, teaching, and the freezing of the Androscoggin River. Shortly after eight, Aidan excused himself and ascended to his room. T couldn't help smiling. "He's like the prototype seven-year-old, the way kids his age were meant to be."

"Don't put him on too high a pedestal. He has his moments."

"Is it difficult for a single mom to raise a boy?"

Faye rolled the teacup in her hands. "Not yet. But we take it a day at a time. I put him on the waiting list for the Big Brother Program, but they said it might take two years to find a volunteer. That's how many boys there are."

"You're doing a fantastic job."

"As I said, he's got a good center. I think he gets it from his father."

"Is this an opening to talk about his dad?"

"No secrets here. No horror stories. Mel died three years ago. Just like that. No warnings. He was a gym rat and a vegan."

"I'm sorry."

"Oh, so am I. He was a good man." Faye paused. "And I think that's the highest praise one can offer anybody. They were good. So, any word from the administration about the suit?"

"Not yet. And I should emphasize that there's no suit yet, just a suggestion of one."

"Do you want to know what I heard?"

"You heard something?"

Faye reached over to a side table and retrieved an envelope. "This came today."

T took the missive and opened the single page.

Dear Adjunct Instructor Mundy:

Please be advised that there are certain employment jeopardies in involving yourself in ongoing institutional legal matters. In order to allow the administration of Skowhegan College to proceed in the best interests of students, faculty, and staff, we must direct that you terminate your activity relevant to any matters involving Professor Tymoteusz Tarnaszewski. Please trust that the relationship between Professor Tarnaszewski and Skowhegan College is being negotiated in good faith. I also trust that you will not share this communication.

Thanking you for your cooperation,
Nedly Trumbull,
President

T handed the letter back to Faye. "My God. This is a threat. And now you've shared it with me. How did they find out about your involvement?"

"Oh, who knows? The hills have eyes."

"That's it, then. Faye, don't worry about me. First things first. Please protect yourself and Aidan. Clive and I can handle it."

"Nice try. Look, they're wrong and you're right. I'm already involved. Retreat is not in my nature."

"But it's not something you have to be involved in. I mean, I don't think it will change any outcomes. But now that you've shown me that letter, are you willing to give me a copy?"

Faye retrieved a leaf from the side table. "I'm way ahead of you." She handed it to T.

"Mom!"

Faye checked her watch. "Eight-thirty. He wants to be tucked in. I figure that within a year or two there will be no more tucking in, so I'd better get it while it's hot. I'm coming!"

"No. *T!*"

Faye smiled. "Well, how do you like that? I'm relieved of duty. How do you feel about doing the honors?"

T was chagrined. "Believe it or not, but I've never tucked a child into bed."

"I believe it. There's nothing to it. Go for it, champ. You'll be great. Aidan will guide you."

T ascended the steps with some trepidation. He stopped on the threshold. The boy's room was small but not cramped, with books, potted plants on the windowsill, a model of the solar system hanging from the ceiling, a telescope, and a small desk harboring drawing utensils. Aidan lay in bed with the comforter drawn up to his chin. "Do you want to read to me?"

T was still hovering on the threshold. "Sure. What'll it be?"

Aidan reached under the comforter and pulled out a big, floppy volume. "This. But you have to do the voices."

T entered, took the book, and sat on the edge of the bed. "I love Garfield. Well, here we go."

He didn't think he had it in him, but he managed to conjure a different comic voice for Garfield, Jon Arbuckle, Odie, and Pooky, taking pains to distinguish between Garfield and Nermal. The result: ecstasy. Aidan howled at every voice, and as he howled, T became emboldened to take ever greater liberties with volume, intonation, and comic glosses. Aidan was laughing so hard that Faye came running up the stairs. "What's going on? He's sucking the air out of the room."

T was also laughing. "We're having a great time." He turned to Aidan. "That's probably all for now, Sport." Aidan took the book and slipped it back under the comforter. He lay back and T watched as, moments later, his eyes fluttered shut. Then he was out.

"My gosh. So there is a difference between going to bed and going to sleep. He's dead to the world."

"Kids have a lot of melatonin. It's proof that God does care about parents."

The night ended at the front door. "This has been delightful," said T. "It's been so long since I've laughed. I actually forgot about my situation for a while." A pause. "Until you showed me that letter."

"I don't believe in secrets. And I don't believe the university, or one man, the president, can issue gag orders."

"You're taking a tremendous risk."

"I have to feel that we'll all make it, one way or another."

T brushed her shoulder with his hand before stepping out into the night.

TWENTY-EIGHT

When he awoke, T was still glowing from the previous night. He had felt comfortably at home with Faye and Aidan. He regretted the years he had spent working around her without ever reaching out, without engaging her. Once in his office, he set to the day's activities, but first, he called Clive. "I have a document for you."

"Good, good. I love documents. Lay it on me."

T described Faye's letter, which elicited a whistle from the other end. "Protect it with your life."

"I'll get it to you before the day is out."

Gary Willins appeared at the door. He looked pained. "Sorry, Professor T," he said. "I have to take your laptop."

T wasn't sure he was hearing correctly. "Please repeat."

Gary hovered on the threshold. "I'm sick about this, but it came down from the top. I have to take your laptop. The school says it's their property, and since it's already November…"

T continued to look Gary over. "But I'm teaching an online course. The school knows this. Am I supposed to abandon those students?"

"The administration says you can use the open-access computers in the library cluster."

T hardened. "This is punitive."

"I know," said Gary, "it sucks. But if I don't take your computer, it comes down on me."

"Can I have a few minutes to get my desktop folders onto my thumb drive?"

"I was told to take the computer, period. They specifically said not to give you time to do anything."

T picked up the receiver of his desk phone. "Oh, I have a call. It must be a private call from a student. Probably an emergency. I'll have to ask you to wait outside, to maintain confidentiality. You understand, right?"

Gary winked and stepped back into the hallway, closing the door. T, with the receiver in the crook of his neck, turned to his computer, gathered up his desktop folders, and uploaded them to the Cloud, taking special care with the M file, which he also transferred to his thumb drive, just in case. Then he scrubbed the hard drive. He signaled to Gary. "Here." He handed over the laptop. "But as you said, this sucks."

Gary took the device and regarded it with something resembling reverence. "Yeah, it does."

"Gary, can you tell me who directed you to do this?"

"Yeah, well, nobody told me not to, so it was the dean."

"Roger?"

"Yep."

T again recollected what Roger Olib had said about having a capacity for action. Well, he couldn't spite him that, however mean-spirited this move. "What now?"

"I'm also supposed to give you a message. The dean said that this would be a good time to start sorting your things, moving what you don't need out of your office."

T managed a smile. "But I need everything."

Gary returned the smile. "That's good enough for me. I was told to give you the message, nothing else. Well, I guess that's it for now."

"Thank you. For being so decent."

T's desk looked bereft without his computer occupying its center. It was a nuisance, but also a humiliation to have to compete for a computer station at the library. He put on his parka and left the building. En route, he crossed paths with Magda. "Long time."

"It's been a while."

"How have you been?"

"Busy."

"My least favorite word."

She smiled. "Where are you headed?"

"The library. The school confiscated my laptop. I have to use the community cluster."

Magda's expression dropped. "That's awful."

"No," said T. "Just inconvenient. Bradley Maun pouring acid on himself was awful."

Magda bit her lip.

"A lot has happened since we last spoke." He checked his watch. "Well, let me get going. I've got to tend to my online course."

"Look," said Magda, "if you'd like someone to talk to..."

T chose his words carefully. "I do wish we could talk like two people who once knew each other." Those words hung heavy in the air for a few moments as they stared at each other. Then T continued on his way.

As he had hoped, there were few students in the library so early in the day. He took a chair in front of a computer and logged on. It wasn't so bad. No laptop meant one less thing to lug around. At least he was out in the campus community now. He enjoyed the benign distraction of seeing people coming and going while he worked. Every so often a student came over to him with a question or to simply acknowledge him. The college may have given him an unanticipated gift.

An hour into his work, Praveen Khatri appeared. He took a seat at a computer next to T. "Hey, nice to see you, Praveen. What? Did they take your laptop too?"

"Excuse me? Is that what they did to you? I don't believe it."

T noted the grimness that had overtaken Praveen's face. "Is it really so hard to believe?" And then, "By the way, I hope you're not still holding a vigil outside the provost's office."

The mathematician's expression remained stark. "No. At first, he was angry and frustrated with me. Then, when I returned there to resume my sit-in after the meeting at Clive's house, he invited me in and spoke kindly to me."

"And?"

Praveen now looked pained, his eyes registering grief. "I made a decision to try to intercede. To make peace."

T's radar flashed on. He lowered his voice and leaned toward his colleague. "And how did you go about making peace?"

"I told him about our meeting, and that people were reasonable but determined. I suggested that people needed to talk to each other."

T's heart sank. "Did you by any chance tell him that Faye Mundy was there?"

"Why, yes. Of course."

If it were anyone else but the gentle, inoffensive, well-meaning man sitting beside him, T's anger would have boiled over. "Oh, Praveen," he moaned. "You've put Faye at risk. She's an adjunct with no protections, no benefits, no promises." And then he thought of Aidan.

Praveen's eyes were pleading. "But he told me that everything would be all right now, that he understood and would reach out to the aggrieved parties. This was a good move that I made. Do you agree?"

T was shaking his head. "No, Praveen, I don't agree. I know you meant well, but you've re-armed the enemy. And yes, I know what I just said. The enemy. All I'm trying to do is continue teaching, but the administration is bent on destruction. They're after me, they're after Faye, and, whether you know it or not, they've taken you prisoner."

Praveen winced. "I…I'm eighty-five…"

T welled with pity for the man. "I'm sorry. I didn't mean to unload on you."

"Maybe I should have a word with the provost. I should tell him how disappointed I am in him."

"No. Please don't. Just continue to teach well and enjoy your students. The school needs you."

The old man got up, nodded, and moved slowly away.

T sat back in his chair and knotted his hands behind his neck. "Goddamn."

TWENTY-NINE

"THEY HAVEN'T SAID A damn thing." T paced back and forth from the kitchen to the living room, cell phone plastered to his ear, with Tootsie dogging his every step and meowing, as if in commiseration. "Okay, counselor, so what now?"

Clive was matter-of-fact. "We get a subpoena for all documents related to Bradley Maun. That means everything that Nan and the provost have."

"Nan will scream bloody murder."

"There's no other way. We can't go into court without evidence. We have to prove that others knew about the threat posed by this student but never told you."

"Didn't we put the cart before the horse by informing the administration of our intent to file suit?"

"That was an appropriate move, but yes, a little chancy. It gives them an opportunity to beg off and return things to normal without going to court. But if push comes to shove, we know the evidence exists, if Boats is telling us the truth."

T thought for a moment. "He must be. He was there for the burning of their tablecloth. I trust him."

"So do I. I'll get to work on it today. But hang on tight. They're going to come after you with everything they have."

"They took my laptop today."

"You're kidding. That's pretty petty, but I'm not surprised."

T smiled into the phone when he considered the consonance of "pretty petty." "There's more. I saw Praveen today. He went rogue and tried to patch things up with the provost. He's the one who told him that Faye was involved in our little conclave."

"Oops. We've got to prevent these ground fires. Damage control makes us look like amateurs."

"I am an amateur when it comes to legal matters."

"That's why I'm here." And then, "This will eventually make it into the papers. That's when the fireworks will really start because the administration will have to devote resources to defending itself in public. And the public itself will take sides. Are you prepared for nasty phone calls and death threats?"

"Clive, who could be prepared for death threats?"

"Let me rephrase. Are you strong enough to withstand death threats?"

"I don't think anyone is going to threaten my life."

"Famous last words. I once wrote a letter to the editor suggesting a per-bag fee for garbage pick-up. Some concerned citizen called me and threatened to burn my house down."

"Isn't what we're doing more esoteric? Who in the community would care or understand anything about trigger warnings?"

"Again, famous last words. Stand by."

When T got to his office the first thing he noticed was how off-routine he felt without his laptop. Tending his email was normally the first thing he did. Now he would have to trudge over to the library. But hey, it was exercise, and after all, there had been life before computers. In fact, it was a life that seemed sweet by comparison with what he was experiencing now.

And so the day would run as follows: go to the library, correct assignments for his online Biology of Cancer course, give his Introductory Biology lecture, teach the associated lab, have lunch, take a walk around campus, and continue to be thankful that Bradley Maun was no longer sitting in front of him contemplating his next mayhem. In light of these grace notes, it seemed inevitable that something would occur to keep the pendulum from swinging too far toward normalcy.

Before heading off to the library T took time at his desk, going over some notes in longhand when the door flew open. There, on the threshold, stood Roger Olib, looking oddly inflated, his scalp red under his sparse gray hair, his face red, his barrel chest heaving. He looked ready to kill. "Tarnaszewski!" he barked.

T was intent on being reserved, measured, and thoughtful. "I wish you had knocked."

"The elevator is broken and I had to climb steps!"

T looked on from his seated position as the man continued to heave. He wanted to remark, "Survival of the fittest," but he hung fire. "I thought Facilities had put in a work order." He indicated a chair. The dean plopped himself down and emptied his lungs with a protracted wheeze. He seemed to be struggling to gather himself. T considered how difficult this must be for a self-styled man of action. A doer. A maker. "I don't think you've ever been to my office."

"And I can promise you won't ever see me in your office again. I expect us to resolve our situation here. Now. This minute."

T cocked his head to the side. "Please tell me what the situation is, as you see it."

Roger Olib narrowed his eyes and looked T over from top to toe as if trying to get the measure of the man. "Let's cut the bullshit. I'm talking about this intent to sue."

T was mindful of Clive's counsel to watch his words. But he didn't see any danger in acknowledging known facts. "What would you like to know?"

Roger Olib looked like he had been punched in the face. With his hands on his thighs, he pushed himself back, then rocked forward again. "*Know*? We don't want to know anything. We want you to stop this nonsense. Break it off. Kill it."

"And go gentle into that good night?"

"Hmm? What's that? What night? What are you talking about?"

"Dean, let's say I call off the suit. Then what? What happens to me?"

Roger Olib brought a hand to his chin and rubbed. He leaned back. "The college is prepared to offer you a package."

"A package?"

"Yes. A one-time offer. A package. A year's pay. With benefits, of course. The whole shebang."

"For doing what?"

For the first time the dean smiled, and it was a triumphant smile. He brought up his hands like an evangelist who had arrived at the river. "That's the beauty of it. For doing nothing."

T nodded. "Oh, I see. You want to pay me off."

The redness, the bloating, had returned to the dean's face. He appeared to be grappling with some internal force. His next words came out as a growl. "I climbed steps," he said. "I came here. I put out my hand..."

"You took my laptop. You made it more difficult for me to do my job. You entered without knocking."

That was it. The dean heaved his bulk to his feet and threw out an accusing finger. For a moment he listed, unsteady. "Listen here, you little sonofabitch..."

Little? T got up and loomed a good five inches over the dean's head. He made a point of looking down at him. "I'm not interested in your offer. I don't take bribes. I leave corruption to those who run this place."

Roger Olib balled his fists. T leaned forward as if inviting the blows. "Please leave. You'll find the descent less strenuous than the climb."

"How dare you! You want action? You'll get action!" As he said this he made a chopping gesture into one of his palms.

"I'm still asking you to leave. If you threaten me again I'll call security and I think I can guarantee that Gary Willins is more than a match for you."

The dean's fury was palpable. T feared that he would have a heart attack right then and there. He had never seen a man flush so blisteringly red, the veins in his neck and forehead bulging. He watched as he stormed out, headed down the hallway, and looked about for the stairwell. Finding it, he disappeared. T sat down and put his head in his hands, his heart racing. That was brutal. Is that what Clive meant when he said they would be coming at him with everything they had? He was exhausted from enforcing his reserve, when what he wanted to do was scream back at the dean, even, God help him, pummel the man. Maybe Clive was right. Maybe he didn't have the fortitude to withstand death threats. And if the dean of a college was capable of such pointed rage, then certainly there were members of the community at large, who were unknown entities and included a range of types, who would have no reservations about crying havoc and letting slip the dogs of war.

THIRTY

Two more days ticked away. T found himself tucked more deeply into November, a month that traditionally had a feel of haste and urgency. It was, after all, the prelude to December—semester's end—and it harbored the Thanksgiving break, toward which the students lunged with all their little hearts. The result was a sense that business had become a collective rush for the finish line.

Despite everything Clive had told him about the hornets' nest they were kicking, he was still unprepared for the call he received at home on his cell, just as he was about to prepare supper. The invective poured forth breathlessly. Hell, indeed, had no fury like a woman scorned.

"How could you!" Nan screamed. "A subpoena! For protected information! Now what am I supposed to do?"

T tried to answer the question but was immediately cut off. "Shut up! Don't talk to me!"

"What would you like me to do?"

"I said not to talk to me. What do I want you to do? Call off this subpoena. Call off this lawsuit."

The wheels in T's head were turning apace. He needed to be very careful here. He was in a position to hurt Nan, damage her career, if he divulged that he knew about her dalliance with the provost, to whom she had likely freely confided the same information she was so protective about now. "Can we discuss this calmly? You're a psychologist, for God's sake."

"A psychologist?" she shouted. "That should be an excuse?"

"I would think that…"

"Shut up!"

"Okay."

T put the phone on speaker, placed it next to his cup of tea, sat down at the kitchen table, and pulled Tootsie onto his lap. He had been neglecting her as of late, so he stroked her coat in tandem with Nan's rants. He glanced at the clock. Six-fifteen. In the ensuing minutes, Nan accused him of everything from disloyalty to lack of professionalism to character assassination to sedition. This gave T an opening to peep, "Sedition?"

"Shut up!"

At six forty-five she was still screaming, but the accusations were now punctuated with lamentations about missed professional opportunities, underappreciation, and personal aspirations for the mark she hoped to make with her hidden brain theory, and now T was conspiring with that "lummox" Clive to ruin everything. By seven PM she was growing hoarse. T heard her pause to gulp water. Then she erupted, "Say something!"

"You knew."

"What?"

T strategized that staccato would be his best chance of getting a word in edgewise.

"You knew."

"What?"

"Bradley Maun was a danger."

"You…"

"Kept it to yourself."

"How…"

"He endangered other people."

He had lit the fuse anew. He should have known that someone with Nan's prodigious energy would be able to sustain a filibuster of execration. He re-set the clock, put Tootsie down, sat back, and continued to listen. That's what Clive had advised. He should do no more than listen. By seven-thirty, he could hear only a breathless heaving. "Nan?"

"I've had it," she said. "You're not the only thing I have to worry about. I have my clients, my courses, my committees, the papers I'm writing…"

T felt the strongest impulse to add to the list, "Your provost." But instead, he said, quietly and clearly, "You know, Nan, you're always busy, but you never have anything to say. I find that incredibly sad."

It was almost imperceptible, but it was unmistakably there. She was crying. Another impulse arose, this time to say that he was sorry. But he wasn't sorry. Not really. However, he was thinking ahead to what Nan's reaction would be when the provost received his subpoena. What would she do then? Was she capable of a death threat? Or, more grimly, carrying one out? According to Boats, hadn't she contemplated getting a gun?

THIRTY-ONE

T WAS ACHING, LITERALLY aching, from his twin encounters with the dean and Nan. It felt like a conflagration and he was trying to remember the directives he had learned in elementary school in the event of fire. One should get down on the floor and crawl beneath the level of the smoke. But first and foremost, get out of the building. Well, T already felt that he was crawling under the weight of the assaults that had come his way, and he knew they were only preludes. But what did it mean to get out of the building? If he threw up his hands and said, "I've had enough. I'm leaving," everything would immediately dissipate. Bradley Maun would go on his merry way, the administration would turn to other concerns, Nan would re-immerse herself in the pursuit of her brain vesicles, and Faye would continue to be the diligent adjunct she had proven herself to be. Yes, it was true—his entire world could be returned to prologue if he simply walked away.

T had gotten up early so he could call Clive and tell him about Roger and Nan while the details were fresh. The counselor listened patiently, humming and smacking his lips by turns. "Yes, yes, very predictable. Very typical. But we've set a large and very heavy wheel in motion. It has a lot of momentum and must be allowed to turn."

Clive had once again waxed poetic, and T wasn't sure what to make of this aspect of his personality. He eventually decided that he approved of it because it showed that the man had perspective and wasn't, like the dean, all action and impulse. In fact, T felt that Clive was the moderating influence in this whole business; he himself sometimes wanted to stand in an open field and scream.

"I made my entries in my M file. It's getting to be quite the dossier."

"And we will make good use of it. Be sure to send me a copy ASAP. We can update it as we go."

"Okay."

"For now, I have to tell you to prepare yourself for the next volley."

"Hmm?"

"The provost should receive his subpoena today."

"Things are moving fast."

Clive concurred. "This is Maine, not Manhattan. This judge has time to tie flies and entertain his grandson. I think he even knits between cases."

"You're kidding."

"Of course I am. But only about the knitting. He ties flies. But he's fully invested in this case. I have to tell you that he doesn't particularly like professors—something about a bad experience as an undergrad—but he truly detests college administrators."

"Let's keep this to ourselves."

It was a truism that, once shit is in the air, it doesn't take long to hit the fan. T managed to make it in peace through most of his day. He taught, corrected some papers, attended a meeting of the Technology Funds Committee, and spent some time in the library tending his online course. A student came by his office for extra help. But at precisely four o'clock his phone rang. The caller i.d. showed the provost's number. It rang a second time, and T continued to stare at the thing. Three rings, then four. After five rings it would go to voicemail. Why postpone the inevitable?

"Don't tell me you don't know who this is."

"I do know, Provost."

"I understand that Dean Olib has already visited your office."

"Yes."

"Then why have I received a subpoena?"

T realized how quickly this conversation could go over a cliff. He was grateful for the default Clive had given him. "That's a question best directed to my attorney."

There was a low groan at the other end of the line. T kept the receiver plastered to his ear. The provost erupted again. "What makes you think I have any information about Bradley Maun that could be useful to you?"

"I think that's what the subpoena is meant to determine. Again, my counsel would be the person to answer your questions."

"I knew nothing about this student's propensity for harm."

T seized a sheet of paper and began to scribble. "Again," he said, dividing his attention between the phone and paper, "this is now a legal matter. Please understand that I have representation and am obligated to defer to my attorney."

It was as if he could hear the provost ruminating. The man twice began to speak but retracted his syllables. Then he redirected. "It's my understanding that the dean offered you a very, very generous package."

"That is correct. I don't deny it."

"And you declined?"

"I'm sure you know that I did."

"Why on earth, man? He put cash in your hand and you burned it. Poof! Up in smoke." Recouping his ground, "But…but with my intercession, I'm sure the offer could be renewed."

T was struck by the provost's effort to sound reasonable. There was a pronounced desperation in his voice as if his future depended on his success in bringing T around.

"I…I'm just baffled, Professor. Help me. Help me to understand why you're doing this."

Any lengthy reiteration of his reasoning would risk too many pitfalls, too many opportunities for a *Gotcha!* But he did venture, "You make it sound as if it's something I'm doing to you personally. I'm not. When the suit is filed everything will be clear."

The provost squealed, "Suit? You're filing a suit?"

The call was moving into the realm of the surreal. "Provost, what do you think all this is about? Subpoenas aren't issued unless a lawsuit is being contemplated."

"Oh, you poor, poor man. You have no idea what you're involving yourself in."

What was this, then? An expression of empathy? A threat? Again, T was hesitant to address the enigmatic statement. "I have nothing else to say."

The provost, hard as rock, "Well, you asked for it, then."

T felt his ire rising. "No, Provost, the subpoena is asking for it. My understanding of legal matters is that it's best to comply. Now, I'm going to allow you to hang up before I do."

Oddly, the provost didn't hang up. He remained on the line, leaving T to count his breath sounds. Then, after some moments, T gently laid the receiver in its cradle. He looked over his notes, written in such haste. There it was. He circled it. That one diagnostic line the provost had uttered. *I knew nothing about this student's propensity for harm.*

If he had known nothing about it, how did he know that a *propensity* for harm existed?

T went to the library, updated his M file, and then stepped outside to call Clive on his cell. The counselor listened carefully. "Well, it could have gone worse. He wanted to see how much wiggle room they had. You did well."

"So what happens now?"

"Let's see what the subpoenas uncover. I'll read the information and then get back to you."

"So what should I do in the meantime?"

"I understand that snow is forecast this evening. Be careful driving."

"I'm always careful."

THIRTY-TWO

CLIVE WAS CORRECT ABOUT the forecast. By early evening big, flat flakes were cascading to earth, so gently and evenly spaced as to suggest choreography. It was just cold enough for them to "stick," and within a very short while all was sparsely adorned with a crystalline white duck down. T stood by the living room window, cup of steaming tea in hand, and regarded the scene. "Very pretty, very pretty," he murmured. He realized that the promise of snow, and cold, was what conjured an image of Maine as forbidding in the minds of many who had never visited the place. When he got his job at Skowhegan, his mother had brought a hand to her mouth and gasped, "All the way up there? You'll freeze to death."

T smiled when he recalled that response. Just as he was raising the tea to his lips his cell rang. Praveen. Of all people. "This is a surprise."

"I'm calling to check on you. I hope you are well."

"That's nice of you, Praveen. Yes, I'm well. Steady as she goes. How about you?"

"I'm actually in your neighborhood. Would it be possible for me to pay a brief visit?"

Praveen had never been to his house. He must have gone out of his way to learn the address. "Sure. Okay. The tea is on."

"I'll be there shortly."

T stoked the woodstove in the living room. It would be his first fire of the season. He worked apace to arrange the newspaper, kindling, and a few stout sticks. He ignited the pile, and it went up gloriously.

T smiled when he recalled an exchange student from Cameroon—a lovely young man—who had once visited. When he saw the woodstove blazing, he stopped and stared at it. "Is such a thing possible?" he had asked, his voice full of wonder. "In the middle of a house? Fire in a box!"

The bell rang. Tootsie ran ahead of T and meowed at the door. When T opened it, Praveen was standing in the glow of the porch light, studded with snowflakes. "Believe it or not," he said, "but I love winter."

"It's not even winter yet."

Praveen came in and lifted his feet out of his boots. T took his coat and scarf, but he kept his hat on. "Thank you."

"How about tea?"

"You're very kind, but no. I won't be staying long."

T gestured toward the sofa, which Praveen examined for a moment as if seeking out an appropriate vantage point. T sat in an easy chair on the opposite side of the room. His colleague glanced about at T's books, an Edward Hopper print of a sailboat on the wall, and a tapestry T and Olivia had received from an appreciative Colombian student. "This is a very warm room."

"Wait until the stove gets going. It'll turn you right out." Praveen didn't get it, so silence reigned for a long moment. "So what brings you out on a night like this?"

Praveen seemed uncomfortable. He leaned forward on the sofa. He took off his knit hat and began to rotate it in his hands. "It is what friends do. I am worried about you."

T was intrigued. "Tell me what worries you." Yes, this was the way to go. Don't volunteer anything. Find out what's bothering the other guy.

"There is a rumor that the college offered you a way out."

T brought a finger to his lips and examined Praveen. "With all due respect, my dear friend, how would you know such a thing?"

"As I said, it's a rumor."

"Rumors have authors. Who told you I was offered a package?" T struggled to remove any hard edges from his voice.

"Is it true?"

"How important is it that you know whether it's true or not?"

"Can we assume that it's true?"

T readjusted his position in his chair. He sat back, rolling the teacup in his hands. "Praveen, why are you here? Did someone send you?"

T had calculated correctly that Praveen couldn't hold up under interrogation. The old man hung his head for a moment and then raised it. "They seem to see me as a useful go-between. They asked that I intercede."

"To ask me to do what?"

"Accept the package."

T leaned back and regarded Praveen thoughtfully. If he had no wish to hurt Bradley Maun, how much less was his desire to hurt this well-meaning man, this friend, who, one way or another, was near the end of his career. But he had to ask, "Praveen, did they offer you a package as well?"

The mathematician's eyes grew moist. He peeped, "More."

T raised his eyebrows. "More?" And then, mischievously, "Did they offer you a million dollars?"

"More valuable."

T felt off-balance. What kind of a game was this? "The next order of magnitude would be a billion. Now, you're the mathematician, so you tell me."

Praveen puffed out the words. "My wife. Without mentioning her unique immigration needs, the college has offered her a position. She would get a visa..."

"I see."

"I'm feeling ashamed."

T saw no harm in letting Praveen marinate in his mortification for a long moment. It wasn't his fault that he couldn't see that he was being used. Finally, "Praveen, I feel bad for you. Do you want to see me give in to the administration so that things will be easier for you?" T immediately saw how cruel this was, and yet there didn't seem to be any other option. Crystal clarity was at stake.

"You are correct."

"I never should have involved you in my situation in the first place."

"Tempt not a desperate man."

"Excuse me?"

Praveen smiled ruefully. "Romeo and Juliet. Tempt not a desperate man."

"Are you desperate?"

Praveen seemed to brighten. He looked directly at T. "I have spent my life resisting temptation. Maybe I no longer have the strength. But things are clearer now. Thank you. I know what I have to do."

"And what is that?"

He nodded, smiling. "This you must leave up to me. Do you agree?"

"I might if I knew what I was agreeing to."

Praveen got up and drew his hat over his ears. "I'm glad we had this conversation."

"I don't feel better for it. I feel that I've let you down."

"Actually, you've helped me. I almost made a dreadful mistake." And then, darkly, "They are going to crucify you."

"They are going to try."

"Goodbye, my friend."

T watched from the window as Praveen made his way to his car, moving in small, measured steps through the fresh snow. He watched as he unlocked the door, knocked the snow from his boots, got in, started the vehicle, and spent a few moments blowing warm air through his cupped hands. Each movement was a conscious one, deliberate, as if every moment were too precious to let go of.

THIRTY-THREE

"Wow, THIS IS A surprise."

Aidan brightened as well. He ran up to T but stopped short of an embrace.

"He's with me today," said Faye as she rummaged in a cabinet in the prep lab. "There was a bomb threat at his school, and so…"

"Welcome to America."

"They said it was one of our students."

"One of ours?"

"Yeah. But no name yet."

Aidan was still standing close to T, looking up at him, his eyes bright. "I love your lab."

T tousled the boy's hair. He looked toward Faye. "What are you up to now?"

"Just scrambling to get to my Human Bio class." She glanced at the wall clock. "My God. Five minutes. You ready to run, Aidan?"

T looked up from the boy. "Leave him here with me. I can show him how to mix pH solutions."

The boy yipped.

Faye sighed. "I'm not even going to feign protest. You got yourself a deal." A moment's pause. "Deal? Ha. What are you getting out of it?"

"A chance to work with a promising student."

Faye hurried on her way. Aidan rallied his enthusiasm. "Just the two of us," he said.

For the next hour, T mentored Aidan along in the formulation of pH solutions for his upcoming lab. The boy was a quick study with an unusual level of focus for a seven-year-old. He rose to the challenge of the precision required for mixing the chemicals. "I couldn't have done it better myself."

Aidan glowed. "What do we do next?"

T checked his watch. "Do you like hot chocolate?"

"Yes!"

The two men set out for the union. The day was cold but clear, the trees bereft of their leaves now. Still, every detail of identifiable nature was grist for Aidan's curiosity: a bracket fungus on the side of a birch, lichens growing on a downed branch, a chickadee, a smooth stone... T realized that in observing the boy he was looking at himself at the same age. Nan Hays had once given a lecture in which she described children as "animals" who could be domesticated only by applying the discipline of education and, presumably, brain emancipation. But this didn't sound right. Aidan was demonstrating that children were not animals. If anything, they were learning machines.

The cafeteria in the union was busy that morning. T and Aidan found a table by a large window, where the boy could watch birds hopping about a feeder suspended from the branch of a crabapple tree. For all his curiosity and verve, Aidan also had a capacity for quiet. He didn't chatter. T looked on as he broke off chunks of his chocolate chip cookie and dipped them into the steaming cocoa. "This is the best way to get both at the same time." T had never had much contact with children and, at this stage of the game, was pleasantly surprised to discover that he found their company enjoyable. Well, at least this particular child. But how would it be if the kid were a hellion?

"So who's this?"

Magda's aspect was pleasant, smiling. She was the last person T expected to see. He found himself hesitating. "Aidan," he finally blurted, and the boy looked up. "No, I mean, this is Aidan. Faye's son."

Magda stood at the edge of their table, her fixed smile dimming. "Oh. So you're watching her kid now?" A failed attempt to sound facetious.

It was that *now* that stuck in him like a cruel hook. T was determined not to play along. “His school is closed today. Bomb threat. They say it was one of our students.”

This seemed to sober Magda. “One of ours? Who?”

“I don’t know. I expect it will come out in the news.”

Magda hovered for a long moment. And then, “Well, I have to run.”

“Nice to see you,” said T. Aidan looked up and smiled. “Me too. Nice to meet you.” Then he returned to his cookie and cocoa.

By the time the two returned to the lab Faye was back from her class. Aidan ran up to her and gave a full report.

“Hot chocolate? I’ve been working here for years and nobody’s ever given me hot chocolate.”

T smiled. “Then you’re overdue.” He would have enjoyed further banter, but he had something on his mind. Excusing himself, he found a quiet corner and called the registrar. He quickly had the information he was looking for. “No, Professor T, Bradley Maun is no longer a student here. He withdrew from all his courses.”

T hung on the line. “Withdrew?” he echoed. “Or was he withdrawn?”

“The student did not initiate the withdrawal.”

“Thank you.”

T was not quite beset, but he became pensive. He called Clive. “You hear about this bomb threat?”

“It just hit the news.”

“They’re saying it was one of our students. You don’t think…”

Clive hummed. “Well, anything is possible.”

“Bradley Maun has been dismissed from the school.”

“Another turn of the screw.” And then, “I was about to call you. I have the information we subpoenaed.”

“And?”

“And they knew. Nan’s notes, as you might expect, are thorough-going. She didn’t miss a detail. The flaming tablecloth is in there. And so much more. Bradley Maun wanted her to vouch for his mental state so he could buy a gun.”

“A gun!”

“That’s just one tidbit. This document is a profile of someone who seemed to spend his every waking hour plotting mayhem. T, you’re lucky to be alive. Bradley Maun is quite capable, according to Nan, of doing grievous harm. We have the provost's notes as well. They're like a transcription and condensation of Nan's. And now that we know the provost knew, well, this thing is like a virus. It makes me wonder about the dean. And the president."

"My God…"

"Be strong. This is going to be a rough day. You're in the spotlight now. Stay calm and continue to take notes."

T drew a deep breath. "So this is it, then."

"Now things will get even more interesting."

T told Clive about Praveen's visit.

"It doesn't surprise me. They're exploring every possible angle to get to you. Don't be surprised if they hold your cat for ransom."

"Funny."

"T, now that the suit is on, the news outlets will pick it up. Recall what I said about the two things that animate institutions?"

"Money and bad publicity."

Clive chuckled. "Good. Your memory will serve us well. Our suit pushes both buttons. But again, seriously, you need to brace yourself."

"What about you?"

Clive chuckled again. "I'm a lawyer, man. I'm already the scum of the earth. I live in the slop. If someone forces my face into the mud it's just a fresh invigoration."

"Did you just think of that, or is it a standard line?"

"Does it matter? We're in this together."

"I'm grateful for everything you've done."

Clive sobered. "There are no guarantees. We could easily lose. Then you'd be gone and they'd turn their guns on me. It could be a bloodbath."

"I don't mind losing my job, so long as I know that I fought to keep it." And then, "But I hate to see you risk your own job because of me."

Clive gave a good-natured shrug. "It's all good. It's good. Just keep your eye on the ball."

"Clive."

"Yes?"

"I've been thinking. Maybe I'm wrong. What if I'm wrong?"

"About what?"

"If I had just installed those trigger warnings I could have gone on teaching the way I always taught. I would have been covered."

Clive moaned. "Oh, T. I said to keep your eye on the ball. Don't get distracted. It's not your failure to give trigger warnings that's the issue here. It's the administration's failure to give you a trigger warning about Bradley Maun. You were put at great risk, not to mention your—our—students."

T was nodding. "Got it."

"I expect to hear from you again soon."

"How soon?"

"The administration will have absorbed the impact of the news before long."

"And then?"

"Counterattack."

THIRTY-FOUR

T's LANDLINE RANG JUST as he was about to leave the house. A reporter for the *Bangor Daily News*, looking for a statement. T was taken off guard. Should he be talking to the press? "What kind of statement do you want?"

"What's the issue, as you see it?"

"Wait. Have you already printed something?"

"We're about to go to press. All we have is SKOWHEGAN PROFESSOR SUES COLLEGE FOR NOT GIVING TRIGGER WARNING ABOUT DANGEROUS STUDENT. We could use some explanation. Your point of view."

T asked for the woman's number. "I'll call you right back." He then called Clive. "What should I tell them, if anything?"

"I had anticipated this. Just give them the bare facts. Don't mention any names. And don't condemn the school. If you remember those three things you'll be okay."

T called the reporter and adhered to Clive's guidelines. The woman typed as he spoke. "Good. Got it. Thanks. We'll be in touch if we have further questions."

The phone rang again just as he was going out the door. He decided not to answer it. He still had job obligations, for a few more weeks, anyway. When he got to his office he sat down and worked a little more on his "eccentric professor" essay. He found that this indulgence, this doing something for himself, helped to center him. If his current trajectory continued and he did indeed lose his job, as seemed likely, he would have to rely more heavily on his writing. It was not an unattractive prospect. But he still didn't want to turn to it as a result of professional ignominy.

T went to the library and searched the web for news of the bomb threat. There were several brief articles, but all were frustratingly bereft of specifics. The threat had been vague, and the individual was still not being named. And then, a news tidbit that floored him: VETERAN PROFESSOR RETIRES FROM SKOWHEGAN COLLEGE.

Praveen. Effective the end of the semester he would be leaving the school. T went into the men's room and called him on his cell. "What's this? If I hadn't stumbled across it on the web I wouldn't have known."

"It is time."

T felt an odd anger. "So let me understand this. Yesterday it wasn't time, but today it's time. And you weren't going to tell me?"

"I'm eighty-five."

"Yes, and in better shape than most fifty-year-olds. It must be all the turmeric you eat."

"You make me laugh."

It occurred to T that he had never seen Praveen laugh. "Can you tell me why you're leaving?"

"They will never be able to use me as an implement again. I will be safe."

"You're safe now."

"I am ashamed of what I did to you."

"Now listen, Praveen. You meant well. You acted out of friendship for me."

"It's time."

"You already said that."

"You must let me go."

Praveen's words sent a chill through T with all the force of remembrance of the last time he had heard them. But he couldn't, at the moment, divide his thoughts between Olivia and Praveen, who was, of course, correct. T had no right to try to bend the decision of someone old enough to be his father. He recalled his ruminations about being dismissed from the school—it would open opportunities for him that his routine and comfort had never allowed him to explore. And yet, how many new horizons existed for an eighty-five-year-old? "What will you do?"

"Return to Sri Lanka."

"Sri Lanka? I thought you were Indian."

"No. When I was born it was known as Ceylon."

Now T felt that he was the one who needed to be forgiven. For not getting to know the man better over the years. He would have at least learned something of Praveen's origins. "I will miss you sorely."

"I am not unhappy with my decision. I will be with my wife again."

"When will I be able to say goodbye to you?"

"We are talking now. Do you think there will be a better time? Do you agree?"

"Goodbye, friend. I will be very disappointed if you don't stay in touch with me."

"I shall."

T spent the rest of the day beset by this casualty of his set-to with the administration. It wasn't, of course, the first. His job was about to evaporate; Bradley Maun had been kicked out of school; his relationships with Magda and Nan had become toxic; and then there was poor Benno. The only light was the imminence of Thanksgiving, which would grant both faculty and students a four-day respite before returning for the semester's denouement.

THIRTY-FIVE

Combustion.

The phone rang with a particular insistence, rousing T from bed. Six A.M. It was the provost, manic. "I've seen the paper!" His screech was so abrasive that T had to pull the receiver from his ear. "So you've seen fit to fight this out in the newspapers."

"Provost, the media scans court filings. It's called freedom of the press."

Lawrence Graveline would not be lectured or mollified. "Now you've done it. Oh, I knew you were a troublemaker from the beginning."

T was nonplussed. If the provost had the least familiarity with his record, he would have recognized him as a model professor. "What do you want me to say?"

"Say? Listen to me. The horse is out of the barn. You want power? You'll get power. Be forewarned."

"I feel like I'm being threatened."

"Feel any goddamn way you want. You've lit a stick of dynamite. Do you think you can just blow it out? First the subpoena, now this. And all because you wouldn't comply with a simple request."

"No, provost. You clearly don't understand the issue. You knew about Bradley Maun. You knew he was a danger. And yet you allowed him to remain in school, a threat to everybody. Do I have to invoke Nan Hays's name here?"

It was a cruel cut that rendered the provost momentarily speechless. Finally—"Nan?"

"Surely you must know that her records regarding Bradley Maun were subpoenaed as well."

"How dare you tell me what I must know."

T sensed that the man was becoming unhinged. How to disengage from this unproductive conversation? "I have to go to work."

"Work?" echoed the provost, his voice weak and pathetic, as if he were examining the word in his head. "What is work if not a distraction..." His voice trailed off.

"I have to go."

Rallying now. "You don't know what you've done."

T thought it a peculiar comment. His curiosity moved him to ask, "Please tell me what I've done."

The provost's response was incongruous. "Do you know what ignominy is?"

"I'm an educated man."

"Ignominy. Ignominious. Obloquy. Odium..." His voice trailed off again.

"Provost?"

"It's out of my hands. I offered you a way out. You slapped the olive branch away. My gesture of good will."

Good will? T thought it best not to reply. He hovered silently on the line. He could hear the provost's panting, almost a gasping. Finally, out of concern for the welfare of another human being, he asked, "Provost? Are you all right?"

"It's out of my hands."

When T got to school Faye was waiting by his office door. "Oh, T," she mourned. She put her arms around him and rested her head against his chest. Then she drew back. "That's to give you a bit of my energy. You're going to need it."

"I'll take all the help I can get."

"I saw the newspaper article. And the story was on TV as well."

"And?"

"And I think it was clear and concise. I think it put you in a good light. A heroic light."

T winced. "I don't want to be a hero. I don't want to be thought of as a hero."

"Oh, you'll have your detractors. Don't worry. But you know whose side I'm on."

"I wish there weren't any sides."

"You're such a purist. Do you have class today?"

"Yes, in about thirty minutes."

"Let's see what your students think."

T walked into a room that was alive with chatter. Every head turned to him, their eyes pleading. T put up his hands. "Can I assume all of you know what's going on?"

There was universal assent.

"All I ask is that you be patient while the legal process plays out."

A young woman spoke up. "Are you going to lose your job?"

"I hope to preserve it."

A murmur passed through the room. A young man: "Should we write letters?"

T shook his head. "I don't expect all of you to agree with any position I've taken, and I respect the differences of opinion that might be present here. Just know that I feel I am acting in your best interest as well as mine."

The silence in the room was abject. T looked from face to face. Their desire to know more was palpable, but he had no intention of using these students in any way, of rallying an army. As much as possible, he had to bear up alone. "Let's try to be cheerful," he finally said. "Where did we leave off last week?"

It was a difficult lecture. Plodding. Their hearts and minds were elsewhere. At the end of class half of them gathered around his desk to offer encouragement. One young man uttered, "Bradley Maun," but T shushed him.

He was never so happy to get back to his office, his fortress of solitude. He sat down, bundled his parka up for a pillow, placed it on his desk, and laid his head down.

He wouldn't have believed sleep to be possible, but he quickly drifted off, and when he did, Olivia precipitated, walking toward him from the garden, her fingers caressing milkweed in bloom as she strode in long, slow, languid steps. Within his dream, T knew he was dreaming, and as such, he found himself wishing he would never wake.

THIRTY-SIX

How long had he napped? He was upended from checking his watch by the shadow that fell over him.

"I apologize for not knocking."

T awoke precipitously. He sat up and raised his eyes to the face looking down at him. "May I sit?"

T nodded dumbly and watched as President Nedly Trumbull turned and quietly closed the door behind him. Then he took up the chair opposite T, who watched him closely, his every studied move. The president maneuvered in the space like a man unfamiliar with doors, doorknobs, and chairs and was fascinated by the existence of such objects. "How long has the elevator been out of order?" he asked in a tone of presumed familiarity.

"Too long." The image of Olivia in the field of milkweed was still occupying his thoughts.

"I had to climb the stairs."

T nodded.

"Do you know why I'm here?"

What T found shocking about the moment was not the fact of the president's presence, but his uncharacteristic eye contact. For the first time, he noticed that the man's eyes were an intense, steely blue. But everything else was in order—the drawn features, the ashen aspect, the long wisps of gray hair brushed back behind his ears, the red bowtie. "I can imagine."

"I'm not here to chastise you. Or to bribe you. Or to offer you a so-called way out. I'm here to tell you that the trustees have been roused from their dark den and are acting swiftly."

"The trustees? Swiftly?"

"Yes. For such a large beast, the board is capable of animating its bulk with alarming speed when necessary." The president's words were calm and clear, with no hint of asperity, as if he were confiding in a friend over a stiff drink. "Your attorney, Professor Gridley, showed them all the information he's gathered and has won them over."

It was not lost on T that the president referred to Clive as "Professor," as if to infer that treason was afoot. "I see." And then, "President Trumbull, do you think I'm wrong in all of this?"

"The trustees also saw the chronology you kept. Very astute. Contemporaneous notes are very persuasive." He was still maintaining strong eye contact. He finally acknowledged T's query. "Wrong? No. Impolitic? Yes. Faculty and administrators occupy different environments and breathe different atmospheres. You as a teacher speak about truth and facts and moral obligations to your students. But we"—thumbing his chest—"think only in terms of appearances and expediency. When you were directed to include trigger warnings, both of these considerations were on our minds, but mostly appearances. Trigger warnings made us look like we were current, and correct, and that we were giving students what they wanted. The public would, of course, approve. And the legislature, with the power of the purse, is part of the public."

T was slowly shaking his head. "President Trumbull, my students never asked for trigger warnings. I think they just wanted me to make the class interesting for them, and to help them understand what we currently believe to be true in science. I think they appreciate that I care about them, and as such, there's not much that they wouldn't do for me."

The president was smiling benevolently but would not be distracted by philosophy. "And Bradley Maun? Didn't he want a trigger warning?"

"Bradley Maun is not a typical representative of student sentiment. I pity the young man, but that doesn't blind me to my observation—my experience—that he is dangerous and in need of help.

And now that we're on the subject, I'd like to emphasize that Nan Hays—Professor Hays—didn't help him by indulging him, hiding the threat he posed, and not sounding the alarm."

The president's smile had melted, his expression now serious. "I can no longer doubt that Mr. Maun is dangerous. I presume you heard the news today."

"News?"

"The other day there was a bomb threat at the elementary school. Bradley Maun made that threat. I have further, proprietary information, as to whom he was targeting. Suffice it to say that it was a little boy. They found a backpack with a crude device. Such is the society in which we live."

T's mind was racing. He was fighting to stay on task, remain focused. "You...you strengthen my case. So what happens now? I guess I still don't know why you're here."

President Trumbull sat back and sighed. "Two things. I wanted to get a closer look at you. I had already read your record and know how esteemed you are among faculty and students." The smile returned. "You would have made a dreadful administrator."

"Thank you."

"And I wanted to say goodbye."

"Goodbye? Goodbyes cut both ways. In a few weeks, according to the provost, I will be history."

"I am sorry to disappoint you, but you're not going anywhere unless you want to. The trustees, in a dramatic gesture, are cleaning house. Very soon there will be some announcements. Provost Graveline and Dean Olib will no longer be associated with Skowhegan College. As for me, there will be boilerplate about wanting to spend more time with my family. In truth, I will find a presidency elsewhere. Scoundrels like me have particular skill sets that are in high demand."

T was speechless at this brazen candor from someone who had no reputation for it. The two men sat looking at each other. Finally, he managed to ask, "And Bradley Maun?"

"The police are seeing to him."

"Nan Hays?"

"She doesn't have a family, so she will be spending more time doing something else, but it won't be at Skowhegan College."

T winced. He knew there was much talent in the woman, and her leaving would be the school's loss. He watched as the president got to his feet and glanced around T's office. "Yes, this is clearly the redoubt of a scientist. I think that, in my next incarnation as an administrator, I'll make better efforts to get to know the faculty."

"Any effort would be appreciated, I'm sure."

"Goodbye."

T put out his hand. President Trumbull examined it, as if, like a door or chair, it was a novel item. He carefully took it, held it for a long moment, and then left.

Was that it, then? T called Clive. It went to voicemail. He threw on his coat and hurried across campus to the science building, looking for Faye. Her class was just ending. Once the students had left he went inside and took her arm. "It's over."

"Over?"

He told her everything that had transpired in his office. "I would never have imagined such a precipitous resolution. Clive must have pressed the right button."

"You spared the school the loss of a million dollars."

His phone rang. He excused himself and leaned against a wall. "Clive? President Trumbull was just in my office." Clive listened patiently as T recounted the meeting, almost word-for-word.

"It all sounds right. Yes, the trustees were flabbergasted. They looked at the evidence and immediately wanted to talk. The news reporting…"

"What you said about bad publicity."

"Yes. I hope you're not sore about losing a million dollars."

"What would I do with a million dollars? This was never about money."

"There will be a little paperwork as follow-up, but for now, carry on. I'll be in touch."

T returned to Faye. "So what now?"

"So dinner now. Can you come over this evening?"

"General Tso's?"
"What else?"

THIRTY-SEVEN

"MY MOM'S GETTING ME an ant farm for my birthday."

T was barely through the door when Aidan was upon him.

"What a great mom."

Aidan beamed.

The supper had a different tone than the previous one. If T had looked up he would have noticed the absence of a dark cloud over his head. He was old enough and wise enough not to conclude that "everything" would be all right now. The next issue, whatever it was, was already in the mail. But he had every intention of indulging himself in this moment of grace and respite. The conversation danced around pleasantries—the weather, the state of learning in the U.S., the prospect of an early spring, the allure of travel to interesting places, and the boon of perspective it granted. It was a conversation whose doors were wide open for Aidan's participation. "Do you like to snow tube?"

T shrugged. "Sure. Where do you go tubing?"

"On the school hill. I'll show you."

"It's a deal." And then, turning to Faye, "You know, this is the best General Tso's chicken I've ever tasted. It's a culinary triumph."

"Thank you. I bought it myself."

After clean-up, Aidan persisted for a while, encased in his own space as he splayed out on the living room floor, paging through a folio of North American mammals while T and Faye enjoyed the quiet, cups of tea, and the warmth of the woodstove. Once again, when the time came, T was called to duty at Aidan's bedside, seeing him safely off to sleep after the requisite preamble of *Garfield*, replete with funny voices.

Back in the living room, T and Faye moved to the sofa. "I feel the strongest impulse to say a few closing words about the recent drama."

Faye regarded him sympathetically. "I'm a big fan of impulse. Let 'er rip."

"I have to admit that I feel better. I feel unburdened. My thoughts, though, are running off in a lot of different directions. I'm grateful that I can continue to teach. I'm grateful for Clive, whom I had long misjudged. I feel sorry for Praveen and his misdirected sentiments, but happy that he may have finally found peace. I regret the loss of Magda's friendship. And there's something in me that feels for Bradley Maun, that fears for his future. But I don't regret the shearing off of the college's administration. There was something truly mean-spirited there, and I think we'll all be better off with a clean start, a more sympathetic start."

Faye had listened to T's retrospective in silence. "I think that covers just about everybody."

He looked at her eyes. "No. I saved the best for last." Having said this, he took her hand. "There are nineteen years between us."

"It's funny, but this is the first time it's occurred to me. Do you think it's an issue?"

"We don't need Praveen the statistician to tell us that I would be the first to go."

"And when you are gone I will miss you bitterly. But listen, my dear, there are no guarantees. Mel was forty-four when he passed. Who knows how long I have? Who knows how long any of us has? When I go into Aidan's room in the morning, all I want to know is that he's breathing, and I'm grateful for another day with him. I have no claim on more than that."

He would not let go of her hand. "There will be more than the three of us. My wife...she still accompanies me. I think of her every day."

"We're all entitled to our thoughts and our memories. But this thing we're contemplating—it will fail only if you believe you can't love more than one person at a time. I'm not in a hurry, if that's any consolation."

T took up her other hand as well and examined both of them as if they were two lovely shells he had found on the beach. "Olivia was a risk-taker, and she was a propulsive force in my life. She was a big fan of opening doors. I'm looking at a door right now. I think I'd like to open it."

At that moment Aidan came down with heavy, deliberate steps. He entered the living room and inserted himself between the two adults. "I can't sleep."

T took up the thread. "Will talking help?"

The boy nodded. "I have a question."

"Shoot."

"Why do things live?"

T pulled the boy close. "That's one of the biggest questions of all. Things live to pass on their genes to their offspring, their children. It's the most important thing that they do."

Aidan yawned. He snuggled deeper into T's chest. A couple of minutes later he was asleep. Faye moved to take him up to bed, but T insisted on doing it, gathering Aidan in his arms. Halfway up the stairs, he turned to Faye and quietly said, "He's breathing," before continuing on, conveying the boy, their replacement, to the threshold of dreamland.

Acknowledgments

I THANK THE FOLLOWING for providing valuable commentary on the manuscript: Patricia Burnes, Mikal Federici, Richard May, Deborah Rogers, Mark Westphal. I couldn't have done it without you.

Made in the USA
Monee, IL
24 September 2023